He bent his head and kissed her.

It was a blatant act of mastery, possessive and angry, yet when Peta tried to resist her body refused to accept the commands of her brain. Peta knew how to defend herself, any other man who'd crowded her like this would have received a fist in the solar plexus followed by a knee in his most sensitive region, but she was lulled into acceptance by treacherous desire.

A low sound in her throat shocked her; sighing, she curled her arms around his neck and gave herself up to the voluptuous delight of his kiss. Her mouth softened beneath the demanding insistence of his kiss, and an overwhelming tide of passion hit her, so fiercely elemental that it shocked her into surrender.

She had no idea how much later Curt lifted his head. Hugely reluctant, she opened her eyes, flinching when the glitter in his was replaced by a taunt.

'I don't think either of us will have to do much acting,' he said with a silky confidence as he let her go.

Robyn Donald has always lived in Northland in New Zealand, initially on her father's stud dairy farm at Warkworth, then in the Bay of Islands, an area of great natural beauty, where she lives today with her husband and an ebullient and mostly Labrador dog. She resigned her teaching position when she found she enjoyed writing romances more, and now spends any time not writing in reading, gardening, travelling, and writing letters to keep up with her two adult children and her friends.

Recent titles by the same author:

THE BILLLIONAIRE'S PASSION
BY ROYAL COMMAND
HIS PREGNANT PRINCESS

THE BLACKMAIL BARGAIN

BY
ROBYN DONALD

MILLS & BOON®

First published in Great Britain 2005
Harlequin Mills & Boon Limited,
Eton House, 18-24 Paradise Road, Richmond, Surrey TW9 1SR

© Robyn Kingston 2005

ISBN 0 263 84132 4

Set in Times Roman 10½ on 12 pt.
01-0305-47567

Printed and bound in Spain
by Litografía Rosés, S.A., Barcelona

PROLOGUE

HARD blue eyes narrowing, Curt McIntosh surveyed his sister. 'All right, you've hedged enough. Tell me straight, is Ian having an affair with this Peta Grey?'

Gillian flushed. 'Don't you look down your nose at me like that! You remind me of Dad when anyone dares to contradict him—high-handed, intolerant and dictatorial!'

His voice stripped of everything but the authority that underpinned its deep tone, Curt stated, 'Nothing you say is convincing in itself. Do you have proof that Ian is sleeping with this woman, or is he just being a good neighbour?'

One glance upwards blocked Gillian's first impetuous response. Not a muscle had moved in Curt's formidable face, compelling in its bold, predatory beauty, but she chose her words carefully. 'I shouldn't have said that—about Dad.'

'It doesn't matter.' He pinned her with a steely gaze. 'And you're still avoiding the subject.'

She flounced around to stare at the view outside his office window. In summer Auckland was thick with jacaranda trees, and the one in the Domain over the busy city road was an airy dome of lilac-purple. Its beauty did nothing to relieve the sick turmoil inside her.

With a spurt of defiance she exclaimed, 'Peta! What a ridiculous name for a girl! I'll bet her father wanted a son.' She gnawed on her lip before finally admitting, 'I know Ian's not just being a good neighbour. There's something else between them.'

Her brother's straight black brow shot up. 'What?'

'Awareness,' she retorted, temper flashing for a second.

'Is this the intuition women are so famous for,' he said drily, 'or is your fear based on something concrete?'

Gillian reined in her anger. It wasn't *fair*; she was four years older than Curt's thirty-two, but the extra years had counted for nothing since he'd turned fifteen and shot up to well over six feet. Those extra inches had given him an edge that his intelligence and tough ruthlessness had honed into a formidable weapon. Although most of the time he was an affectionate brother, when he went into intimidation mode she took notice.

She said unsteadily, 'You might not know much about love, Curt, but don't try to convince me you don't understand sizzle! You were only sixteen when you seduced my best friend, and you haven't been wasting any time since then—'

Shrugging, he broke in, 'Is that all you've got to go on? An awareness of sizzle?'

She flushed at the satirical note in his words and shook her head.

Dispassionately he said, 'It happens, Gillian. It's the way men are; we see a beautiful woman and the hormones begin to stir. An honourable man doesn't follow it up if he's already committed. I've always believed Ian to be honourable.'

'Oh, how you testosterone brigade stick together!' She forced herself to be calm because he distrusted emotional outbursts. Eventually she said in a more temperate voice, 'Curt, I'm Ian's wife. I love him, and I know him very well. Trust me, whatever it is that Ian feels for Peta Grey it's more than a quick, easily forgotten flash of lust. I'd accept that if she was gorgeous, but she's not. She's not even pretty.'

'Then what are you worrying about?' Curt demanded, adding with cool logic, 'Ian's not likely to throw everything away on a plain woman. What does Peta Grey look like?'

'She's striking,' Gillian admitted resentfully, 'if you like tall, broad-shouldered, *strong* women. And that's one of the reasons I'm worried—she's not Ian's type at all. The only times I've ever seen her in anything smarter than a T-shirt and jeans and gumboots have been when we've invited the neighbours around for drinks or a barbecue. She scrubs up pretty well then, but she's so…so *rural*. All she can talk about is her stock and the measly few hectares she calls a farm.'

She paused, then added with bleak honesty, 'Which is more than Ian and I seem to have to talk about now.'

Curt examined her closely. Small and slight, his sister breathed urban sophistication; on her own ground she'd hold all the weapons. 'So what does Ian see in her?'

Eyes glittering with frustrated tears, Gillian snapped, 'She's tall, and I imagine her mouth and green eyes make her sexy in a kind of earthy, land-girl way. Apart from that she's got lovely skin, brown hair usually dragged off her face and tied with string in a ponytail, and a reasonably good figure.'

Curt inspected his sister from the top of her expertly cut hair to the slim Italian shoes on her narrow feet. 'She doesn't sound like competition. Why would Ian fall for her?'

'Oh, you know Ian—he's always had a soft spot for people who work hard. Probably because he had to haul himself up by his bootstraps.' After a short hesitation she said reluctantly, 'And she's a battler—she's only got a few acres besides the land that Ian leased her, but she manages to scrape a living from it.'

Curt had thought nothing of his brother-in-law's decision to lease a small area to his neighbour. Cut off from the rest of the station by a large gully, the land hadn't been fully utilised. Now he wondered why it hadn't occurred to him to suggest it be planted with trees…

He said judicially, 'You're sophisticated enough to know that men don't fall in love with every woman they admire. There must be more than that to it.'

Her desperation showing, she retorted, 'She's at least ten years younger than I am—she can't be much over twenty-three or -four. And a couple of months ago I noticed that whenever he talked about her—which he no longer does, and that's a bad sign too!—something about his voice set every alarm off.' She looked her brother full in the face. 'You're not the only one in the family with good instincts. I know when my marriage is threatened, and believe me, Peta Grey is a threat.'

Curt's brows drew together but he tempered his voice. 'If you want me to do something about it you're going to have to give me proof, Gilly. So far, you haven't.'

She spread her hands in a gesture that held elements of both appeal and despair. Elegant, manicured hands, he noted, with Ian's engagement and wedding rings making a statement on one long finger.

'I don't think they're lovers yet,' she admitted, 'but it's only a matter of time, and I want us out of Northland before—before it happens. A few months ago Ian was talking about a job in Vanuatu managing your rice plantation there. He seemed intrigued…'

The words trailed away as Curt said quietly, 'Gilly, be reasonable. I can't just move him on without some proof that it's necessary. He's doing a good job on Tanekaha; he's hauled the station into profit under budget, and he's a skilful manager of staff.'

Tears welled in her eyes, but even as he found his handkerchief she fought them back with a flare of anger. 'Oh, see for yourself! I hate showing you these—I'm ashamed I even looked at them!—but if you want proof, here it is.'

She groped in her bag, hauled out a couple of photographs and hurled one onto the big desk. '*Now* tell me I've got nothing to worry about!'

Curt picked up the photograph. His brother-in-law stood facing a woman, a hand lifting to her face.

'Check out this one too,' Gillian said savagely, plonking another down on the desk.

If he'd had any doubt at all, the second shot banished it. This time both the people in the picture had turned towards an out-of-focus blur that might have been a bird swooping low, and the guilt stamped on Ian's face would have convinced anyone.

Frowning, he examined the woman's features. Certainly no beauty, but deep in his gut something stirred, a primal appetite that hardened his voice. 'Who took the shots?'

'Hannah Sillitoe—Mandy's daughter. She got a digital camera in her Christmas stocking. Mandy dropped in to see us on their way back to Auckland after the holidays, and of course Hannah spent every moment outside taking photos of anything that would stay still long enough.'

Curt dropped the shiny images onto his desk. 'How did she get these?'

'She thought she saw a native pigeon fly into the big puriri tree by the stockyards. She's an adventurous kid so she climbed the tree, but she couldn't see any sign of the bird. She was on her way down when Ian and Peta came out of the old barn and stopped to talk.' Her hands clenched by her sides. 'Hannah was intrigued by the way the sun caught Peta's hair, so she snapped them. The flash must have startled the pigeon because it swooped from the tree and flew towards them.'

Curt nodded. 'Go on.'

She indicated the second photograph and finished in a voice brittle with humiliation, 'They both swivelled around. Hannah tried to get a picture of the bird, but got that instead. When Mandy saw them she thought I should know what was going on.'

Curt asked brusquely, 'What happened then?'

'Hannah said they went off in different directions.'

He examined the photographs again, reluctantly admitting they were pretty damning evidence. Everything about the two figures shrieked intimacy—their closeness, the way they inclined subtly towards each other, their unconscious mimicry of stance and posture.

And being a man, he could understand what Ian saw in Peta Grey. The faded T-shirt moulded breasts voluptuous enough to stir a eunuch's blood, and beneath the faded jeans her legs were long and lithe. Her coolly enigmatic face challenged the camera, and her mouth was sultry enough to tempt a saint; what would it take to shatter that air of control and release the passion beneath?

Of course, you might find nothing but naked self-interest there.

Anger smouldered to life inside him. 'Does Ian know you've got these?'

'No, and I'm not going to tell him,' Gillian returned with spirit. 'I'm not that stupid.'

Curt noted the way the sun shone on Peta Grey's hair. The elemental fire in the pit of his stomach burned hotter, transmuting into something more complex than anger. When Gillian spoke he had to yank his gaze from the photograph to focus on her.

'Curt, why don't you come up and see for yourself? Believe me, if I'm wrong I'd be so relieved and grateful.'

Her voice broke on the final word and the smile she'd summoned wavered, then tightened into a grimace as she fought back tears. 'I'm sorry to lump you with this, but there's no one else I trust enough. And no one I can talk to.'

Which was his fault; Gilly had supported him when he needed her, and her love and faith had been punished. Neither of them had spoken to their parents for ten years.

Curt slung an arm around her shoulders and drew her against him. She sniffed valiantly, but eventually surrendered to harsh, difficult sobs, clutching his shirt with desperate hands as she gave up the fight for control. Like him, she'd been conditioned to hide her emotions, so she was terrified at this threat to her marriage.

'All right,' he said quietly when her tears began to ease. 'I can come up next week.'

He'd planned a tryst in Tahiti with his current lover, but this was more important.

Mouth quivering, she reached up and kissed his cheek. 'Thank you,' she said soberly. She stepped back and grimaced at his shirt. 'I've made you all wet—and streaked with lipstick. Have you got a spare shirt here?'

'It doesn't matter, but yes, I have.' He lifted her chin and met her eyes. 'If I think you're wrong, what will you do?'

'Find a counsellor, I suppose,' she said drearily. 'I'll need it, because…oh, because things have been going wrong since before Ian noticed Peta Grey.'

'What things?'

Gillian paused. 'Oh, you might as well know everything. Since we found out that the reason I can't get pregnant is an infection I caught in my wild youth. I never pretended to be a virgin when we met, but as long as I didn't rub his face in my love affairs Ian didn't seem to mind. Discovering why I couldn't conceive is rubbing his face in it with a vengeance, Curt.'

'I don't imagine he was a virgin either when he married,' Curt said forcefully.

'No, but he wasn't careless enough to let himself be made sterile. Ian wants children, and once we got the results he started pulling away.' She dragged in a deep breath. 'He blames me, of course. And like all you men, he's possessive.'

'I don't consider myself possessive,' Curt said brusquely. 'I don't share, but that's not possessiveness.'

'You've never loved anyone enough to be possessive.' His sister gave him a trembling smile. 'Ian might even still love me, but he wants a family, and he—he might be looking for someone who can give him one.' She pulled away and finished steadily, 'Someone who isn't infertile because she slept around.'

Astonished, Curt asked, 'Are you telling me that this Peta Grey is a virgin? How do you know?'

'I don't. There has been gossip, but apparently her father was a very controlling man—he didn't let her go out with boys. Her mother was delicate so Peta left school the day she turned sixteen, and acted as nurse, housekeeper and farmhand until her parents were killed in a car accident a few years later.'

'You seem to have been gossiping to a purpose.' Curt's distaste sharpened his voice.

Gillian shrugged. 'I heard you say once, *Know your enemy*. In a way I feel sorry for the girl. She's spent her life on that little farm working all hours of the day and night to survive.' She looked up, entreaty plain in her lovely face. 'I don't wish her any ill; I just don't want her to wreck my marriage.'

'Has it occurred to you that if Ian wants her, you'll be better off without him?' Curt knew it had to be said, even though his bluntness drove the colour from her face. 'He made vows. If he breaks them, will you ever trust him again?'

Trust Curt to voice her worst fear. Gillian had to stop her hands from twisting together in futile terror. 'I need time,' she told him intensely. 'I love him, and if there's any chance that he still loves me I'll fight this—this *fling*. He's a sophisticated mature man, and she's a...well, she's a *nothing*!'

'If he thinks he's in love with her, any hint of interference might persuade him to leave you.'

'You always did make me face consequences,' she said in a low voice, 'and yes, I accept that. If he does leave, I—I don't know what I'll do, but I'll deal with it. It's the wondering and waiting and uncertainty that's tearing me apart.'

'I'm not a miracle worker,' Curt warned her.

'You'll fix it,' she said eagerly. 'You've always done what you set your mind to. I have complete faith in you!'

That, he knew. Her faith had cost her dearly. 'What exactly did you have in mind?'

Gillian rushed on, 'Couldn't you make a play for her? If she's like ninety-eight per cent of womankind she'll fall at your feet in worshipful delight.'

'You grossly overestimate my effect on your sex,' he said drily. 'Is that what you want me to do?'

Her anxious eyes searched his face. 'I—well, probably not. Nobody, especially not Ian, would believe that you'd find a girl like her attractive.' She gave a twisted smile. 'Your preference for beautiful women is too well known. But there must be some way out of this, because I'm certain she's not in love with him.'

'How do you know?' Curt asked ironically. 'And don't tell me it's women's intuition.'

'Ha! That's rich coming from you!' Now that he'd agreed she was confident again, her eyes gleaming and her smile reckless. 'Everyone believes you dragged Dad's sinking firm out of the mire and into the stratosphere with brilliance and sheer force of will, but you told me once that most of the time you followed your gut instinct.'

'And sometimes I ignored it,' he said sardonically.

'Well, intuition's got nothing to do with this. You got to the top because as well as being brutally clever you're good at reading body language,' she said crisply. 'So am I. And her body language tells me Peta Grey is *not* in love with Ian. She wants out of being stuck away on a little farm miles from the nearest village, with no money, no prospects except hard work, and no chance of meeting a decent man. Except married ones!' she finished bitterly.

Curt glanced down at the photographs, his gaze caught and held by Peta Grey's challenging face with its lush, firmly disciplined mouth. His protective affection for Gillian warred with a darker, more subtle instinct that warned him of danger if he didn't keep out of this.

But looking after his sister was a habit too strong to be broken. He leaned over and wrote something in his desk diary. 'All right, I'll see you next week.'

She let out a long sigh. 'Thank you,' she said in a voice that quivered. 'I'll be eternally grateful.'

'I'm not promising anything,' he said abruptly. 'Can I take you out to lunch?'

'I'd love to go out to lunch with you, but I'm already

booked with a couple of old girlfriends. Besides, I bet you've got some high-powered meeting with important people.'

'Guilty,' he agreed, with the rare smile that dazzled even his sister. 'But I'd have cut it short if you needed me.'

She came up to him in a small, scented rush and pulled his head down to kiss his lean cheek, then rested her head on his chest for a second. 'I knew I could rely on you,' she said, and gave him a gallant smile and left.

Frowning, Curt watched her go, then called his secretary. 'Have John Stevens contact me as soon as possible,' he said, hard eyes missing nothing of the traffic heading towards the magnificently columned Museum. Shining like a white temple in the summer sun, Auckland's tribute to its war dead crowned a hill that commanded the city and the harbour.

At any other time he'd look forward to a week on Tanekaha, but even apart from the loss of time with Anna he didn't expect to enjoy this stay. He swivelled and picked up the photographs again, gazing not at his brother-in-law but at the woman so nearly in Ian's arms. The sun shimmered in lazy golden fire across her head; at her feet he could see a hat, as though an ungentle hand had pushed it off.

To make it easier to kiss that sensuous mouth?

Probably; there had been no kiss, but that didn't mean one hadn't been planned.

His mouth compressing, he dropped the photographs as though they burned his fingertips. Think possible gold-digger, he advised himself, and find out everything you can about her so you know which strings to pull.

If he had to he'd even buy her off, although it would

go against the grain. Still, he'd part with anything if it would save Gillian's marriage; apart from his natural affection for his sister, he owed her more than he could ever repay.

CHAPTER ONE

PETA'S head came up sharply. Hoof-beats coming up the hill? Who the hell could it be? Not Ian, who'd be driving his ute. Her mouth tightened into a straight line. So it had to be Curt Blackwell McIntosh—the owner of Tanekaha Station, hunk, tycoon, and adored brother of Gillian Matheson.

A convulsive jerk beneath her hands switched her attention back to the calf.

'Just stay still,' she told it in her most soothing tone while she eased a rope around it, 'and we'll have you out of this mud in no time—oh, *damn*!' as the dog let out a ferocious fusillade of barks.

'Shut up, Laddie,' she roared, but it was too late; thoroughly spooked, the calf found enough energy to thrash around wildly, spattering her with more smelly mud and water and embedding itself even further in the swamp.

Muttering an oath, she lifted its head so that it could breathe, then snapped a curt order to 'Get in behind' at the chastened dog.

If Curt McIntosh was as big as he looked in photographs, he was just the man to help her drag this calf out!

Her mouth relaxed into a scornful smile. 'Not likely,' she told the calf, now quiescent although its eyes were rolling wildly. 'Far too messy for an international magnate. Still, he might send a minion to help.'

17

And that would be fine too, provided the minion wasn't Ian.

She squinted against the sun. Like a storm out of the north, Curt McIntosh and his mount crested the hill and thundered towards her, a single, powerful entity both beautiful and menacing.

An odd chill of apprehension hollowed out her stomach. To quell it, she sniffed, 'Take a good look, Laddie. That's what's known as being born to the saddle!'

But Curt McIntosh hadn't been. He was an Aucklander, and the money that financed his pastoral empire came from the mysterious and inscrutable area of information technology; his firm was a world leader in its field. He might ride like a desert warrior, but his agricultural and pastoral interests were a mere hobby.

Horse and rider changed direction, slowing as they came towards the small patch of swamp. A primitive chill of foreboding shivered across Peta's nerve ends; as well as being a brilliant rider, Curt McIntosh was big. Quelling a crazy urge to abandon the calf and get the hell out of there, she watched the horse ease back into a walk. At least Curt Etc McIntosh and his horse weren't pounding up with a grand flourish that would scare the calf into further suicidal endeavours.

'Of course it's black,' she murmured to the dog bristling with curiosity at her heels. 'Raiders always choose black horses—good for intimidation. Not that he's going to find any loot here, but I bet you an extra dog-biscuit tonight that horse is a stallion.'

She'd heard enough about Curt McIntosh to be very wary; his reputation for ruthlessness had grown along with his fortune, but he'd been ruthless right from the start. Barely out of university, he'd manoeuvred his father out of the family firm in a bitterly fought takeover, dragged the company into profitability, then used its resources to conquer the world.

'The dominant male personified,' she stated beneath her breath. It hurt her pride to remain kneeling in the mud as though waiting for a big strong man to come and rescue her and the calf, but she didn't dare loosen her grip on its slippery hide to grab the rope.

'Hang on, I'll just tie the horse.' A deep voice, cool, authoritative, completely lord-of-the-manor.

It should have set Peta's teeth on edge; instead, it reached inside her and tied knots in her system. Without looking up she called, 'OK.'

Cool; that's all she had to do—act cool. She had no need to feel guilty; for all McIntosh's toughness and brilliance he couldn't know that his brother-in-law had touched her cheek and looked at her with eyes made hot by unwanted desire and need.

Thank heavens for that pigeon in the puriri tree! Its typically tempestuous interruption had stopped him from doing anything they'd both regret.

Until then she'd had no idea that Ian had crossed the invisible line between friendship and attachment. Shocked and alarmed, since then she'd made darned sure that he hadn't caught her alone.

As though her turbulent thoughts had got through to the calf, it suddenly bawled and tried to lever itself further into the sticky clutches of the mud.

Clutching it, she said, 'Calm down, calm down, I'm trying to help you. And Laddie, if you bark again there'll be no snacks for a month!'

Laddie, barely adult and still not fully trained, tried to restrain himself as Peta struggled with the demented calf. Out of the corner of her eye she saw the tall rider come towards her; Laddie gave up on silence and obedience and let rip with another salvo of defiance. The calf thrashed around, and a lump of smelly goo flew up and hit Peta on the jawbone.

Furious with everyone and everything—most of all with herself—she shouted, 'Quiet!' at the dog, wiped the worst of the mud off onto her shoulder, and bent again to the calf.

Still murmuring in her softest, most reassuring tone, Peta ignored the icy emptiness beneath her ribs. It was, she thought bitterly, utterly typical that the landlord she'd never met should find her spattered in mud and dealing with something no respectable farmer would have allowed happen.

It had to be a McIntosh thing. For all her charm, his sister always managed to make her feel at a total disadvantage too.

Silence echoed around her, while the skin on the back of her neck and between her shoulder blades tightened in a primitive warning. Laddie made a soft growling noise in his throat.

'I'll do that,' a deep voice said.

Although she fiercely resented that uncompromising tone, a bolt of awareness streaked down Peta's spine, setting off alarms through her body. As well as that peremptory command, his voice was textured by power and sexual confidence. It set every prejudice she had buzzing in outrage.

Slowly, deliberately, she turned her head and took in the man behind her with one calm, dismissive survey.

At least that was what it was meant to be. Maddeningly, cold blue eyes snared hers before she'd got any further than his face—handsome, superb bone structure—a face where danger rode shotgun on authority.

Damn, she thought helplessly, he is gorgeous! Her throat closed. And up close he was even bigger than she'd suspected, long-legged and lithe, with shoulders that would be a credit to a rugby player. Clear and hard and ruthless, his gaze summoned an instant, protective antagonism.

Curt McIntosh's formidable toughness hammered home her acute vulnerability. Oh, what she'd have given to be able to get to her feet and look him in the eye!

'Thank you,' she said. 'I almost had her out, and then the dog barked—' Shocked, she stopped the excuse before it had time to shame her.

'Just keep her head above the mud.' He picked up the rope she'd been trying to get under the calf's stomach.

Heart contracting in her chest, Peta ran a swift glance over his clothes. Well-worn the checked shirt and faded jeans might be, but they'd been made for his lean body and long, strongly muscled legs. Of course, his sister patronised the best designers.

It was probably this thought that loosened the links of her self-control. 'You'll get covered in mud,' she pointed out.

His smile narrowed into a thin line. Another shivery—icy this time—scudded down Peta's backbone.

'It wouldn't be the first time,' he said. 'I'm not afraid of a bit of dirt, and you're not strong enough to haul it out by yourself.'

True, and why shouldn't he experience first-hand what rural life could be like? 'It needs know-how, not just brute strength.' She summoned a too-sweet smile, inwardly flinching when his eyes turned into ice crystals. 'Although the brute strength will be very useful.'

The calf chose that moment to kick out in a desperate surge forward. Peta made a swift lunge at it, lost her balance and pitched towards the smelly mud. Just before the point of no return, a hard hand grabbed the waistband of her shorts, another scooped beneath her outstretched arms, and with a strength that overwhelmed her Curt McIntosh yanked her back onto firm land.

Gasping, she struggled to control her legs. For one stark second she felt the imprint of every muscle in his hard torso on her back, and the strength of his arm across her breasts. Although the heat storming her body robbed her of breath, strength and wits, instinct kicked in. *Move!* it snapped.

'I—thanks,' she muttered. But when he let her go she stumbled, and he caught her again, this time by the shoulders.

'Are you all right?'

The level detachment of his voice humiliated her. 'Yes, thank you,' she said, striving for her usual crispness.

He loosened his grip and she stepped away. With the imprint of his knuckles burning the skin at her waist, she blurted, 'You've got fast reactions for such a big man.'

Oh, God! How was that for truly sophisticated repartee?

His brows rising, he squatted to reach for the calf. Holding its head above the mud he said, 'I hope this isn't one of my calves.'

A spasm of apprehension tightened her nerves another notch. More mildly she said, 'Yes, it's one of yours. If you can lift her enough to get her belly free of the mud, I'll slide the rope under her.'

Be careful, she told herself as he crouched down beside her. Clamp your mouth on any more gauche remarks, and remember to be suitably impressed by his strength and kindness once the calf's out of the swamp.

This man could make her life extremely difficult. Not only did she lease ten vital hectares from him, but her only income this year was the money she'd earn from that contract. As well, sole access to her land was over one of his farm roads.

With two rescuers, one of them impressively powerful and surprisingly deft, freeing the calf turned out to be ridiculously simple. Curt McIntosh moved well, Peta thought reluctantly as they stood up, and he was in full control of those seriously useful muscles. She was no lightweight, and he'd saved her from falling flat on her face in the mud with an ease that seemed effortless, then hauled the calf free without even breathing hard. Clearly he spent hours in the gym—no, he probably paid a personal trainer megabucks to keep him fit.

Ignoring the odd, tugging sensation in the pit of her stomach, she bent to examine the calf, collapsed now on the ground but trying to get to its feet.

'Where do you want her?' Curt asked, astonishing her by picking up the small animal, apparently not concerned at the liberal coating of mud he'd acquired during the rescue.

Infuriatingly, the calf lay still, as though tamed by the overwhelming force of the man's personality.

And if I believe that, Peta thought ironically, I'm an idiot; the poor thing's too exhausted to wriggle even the tip of its tail.

She'd been silent too long; his brows lifted and to her irritation and disgust her heart quickened in involuntary response. The midsummer sun beat down on them, and she wished fervently she'd worn her old jeans instead of the ragged shorts that displayed altogether too much of her long legs.

'On the back of the ute.' She led the way to the elderly, battered vehicle.

He lowered the calf into the calf-cage on the tray of the ute. 'Will she be all right there?'

'I'll drive carefully,' she said. The manners her mother had been so fussy about compelled her to finish with stiff politeness, 'Thank you. If you hadn't helped I'd have taken much longer to get her out.'

He straightened and stepped back, unsparing eyes searching her face with a cool assessment that abraded her already raw composure. 'So we meet at last, Peta Grey,' he said levelly.

Pulses jumping, she could only say, 'Yes. How do you do?' Mortification burned across the long, lovely sweep of her cheekbones. Bullseye, she thought raggedly; yet another supremely sophisticated bit of repartee!

He smiled, and she almost reeled back in shock. Oh, hell, she thought furiously, he could probably soothe rattlesnakes with that smile—female ones, anyway! 'How do you do?' he replied courteously.

Just stop this idiocy now! she ordered herself. Your heart is not really thudding so loud he can hear it.

But perhaps it was, because when she looked up she saw his eyes rest a second on the soft hollow at the base of her throat. Thoughts and emotions jangling around in turbulent disarray, she went on painstakingly, 'And I believe we'll be seeing each other tomorrow night at your sister's barbecue.'

'I'm looking forward to it,' Curt McIntosh said, somehow managing to turn the conventional response into a threat. He looked around at the paddocks that belonged to him. 'Your lease is up for renewal, I believe.'

It wasn't a question; of course he knew it was due for renegotiation. Foreboding brushed her skin like a cold feather. Seriously unnerved, she evaded his gaze and looked past him to his mount. With lowered head, the big black animal was cautiously inspecting Laddie. 'In a month's time.'

'I'll give you fair warning,' he said, still in that pleasant tone, although now she recognised the steel beneath each word.

Defiantly, she lifted her head to meet his eyes. Cold blue had swallowed up the grey rims, and they were too keen.

The hollowness beneath her ribs expanding into a cold vacuum, Peta braced herself. 'Warning of what?'

Instead of answering Curt McIntosh whistled; Laddie frisked across to his frozen owner while the horse—a gelding, Peta noted tensely, not a stallion—paced with measured strides towards the man who'd summoned it.

He swung up into the saddle and gathered the reins in one lean, mud-stained hand, examining her with an unsparing gaze. She took an involuntary step backwards. Horse and rider seemed to blot out the sun.

All trace of emotion gone from his face, from his voice, Curt said, 'I'm in two minds about renewing it.'

Panic kicked her brutally in the stomach. Peta looked him full in his starkly powerful face and tried to hide the thin note of desperation in her voice. 'Why? It would cost you a lot of money to build a bridge across the gully and link it to the rest of the station.'

He didn't tell her that money was the last thing tycoons lacked, but she saw the glint of mockery in the depths of his eyes when he said negligently, 'That's my worry.'

One glance at that formidable face told her that pleas wouldn't work. Swallowing, she said, 'I was informed that it would be all right...'

Her voice tailed away when she realised that he was

once more looking at the long line of her throat. Her breath blocked her airways. Then he raised his eyes and she had to stop herself from flinching because dark fire flared for a second in the blue depths.

'Then whoever told you that made promises he knew he might not be able to keep. I have plans for this land.'

Without waiting for an answer, he made a soft, chirruping noise. Obediently the gelding picked up its hooves and turned away.

Motionless, her mind darting after thoughts like a terrier after rabbits, Peta watched them go. Of course the children of rich parents had advantages, and learning to ride as well as you could walk was just one of them. She'd never learned; her father hadn't seen the necessity.

But then, he hadn't seen the necessity of a lot of things. After he'd died she'd relied on her neighbours' offers of lifts into Kowhai Bay until she'd learned to drive.

And Curt McIntosh was another dominant male who thought he had a God-given right to make decisions and control people.

Slowly, stiffly, she got into the ute, but once in its stuffy interior she sat with hands gripping the wheel while she stared unseeingly ahead.

On the rare occasions they'd met, Gillian Matheson had spoken of her brother—so strong, so clever, so drop-dead stunning that women fell at his feet! But Gillian was a restless, dissatisfied woman, and often her words had seemed to be aimed at her husband; although Peta had listened politely, she hadn't believed in this paragon. After all, extremely powerful magnates were by definition attractive to women—some women, anyway.

She believed Gillian now.

'Up, Laddie!' she called, patting the seat beside her,

and waited while the delighted dog jumped in. 'Yes, this is a real treat for you, isn't it? Just don't get used to it; the only reason you get to ride in front is because on the tray you'll spook that calf even more.'

Slotting the key into the ute, she turned it, but something about the engine's note brought her brows together. It was missing again. 'Not now,' she breathed, putting the vehicle into gear.

Instead of working in the garden that evening she'd poke around the motor and see what she could find. And if it wasn't something she could fix it would have to wait, because she couldn't afford any repairs this month.

But during the careful trip down to the calf-shed, she wasn't working out what she could do if the knock in the engine was too much for her basic mechanical skills. Her mind dwelt obsessively on Curt McIntosh, whose touch had sent her hormones on a dizzying circuit of every nerve in her body.

And whose relentless authority and aggressive, arrogant masculinity reminded her so much of her father she had to unclench her jaw and rein in a storm of automatic resentment and anger.

He controlled her future.

If he refused to renew the lease she'd have to get rid of her own stock, the ones she was rearing for sale in two years' time to finance a new tractor. Because Ian's calves—Tanekaha's calves, she corrected hastily—were covered by contract, their needs were paramount. Without the leased acreage she had barely enough land to finish them off and send them back in good condition.

But she desperately needed a new tractor. Hers had to be coaxed along, and six months ago the mechanic told her it wasn't going to last much more than a couple of years—if she was lucky.

She braked and got out to open a gate. Without the income from her stock she'd be in real trouble; extra hours pumping petrol at the local service station wouldn't cover the cost of a new tractor.

Swallowing to ease her dry throat, she got back into the ute and took it through the gate. And there was little chance of more casual work at Kowhai Bay; the little holiday resort sank back into lethargy once the hot Northland sun headed for the equator.

After she'd closed the gate behind the ute, she leaned against the top bar and looked out over countryside that swept from the boundary to the coast.

Her smallholding was insignificant in that glorious panorama, yet the land she could see was only a small part of Tanekaha Station. Blue hills inland formed the western boundary, and the land stretched far along the coastline of beaches and stark headlands, shimmering golden-green in the bright heat.

Lovely in a wild, rugged fashion, serene under the midsummer sun, it represented power and wealth. If it came to swords at sunrise, Curt McIntosh had every advantage.

Perhaps she should give up the struggle, sell her land for what she could get, and go and find herself a life.

She bit her lip. All she knew was farming.

'And that's what I like doing,' she said belligerently, swinging back into the vehicle and slamming the door behind her.

Once she'd settled the calf undercover in a temporary pen made of hay bales, she glanced at her watch and went inside.

After a shower and a change of clothes, she went across to the bookshelves that bordered the fireplace, taking down her father's Maori dictionary.

'"Tanekaha",' she read out loud, and laughed ironically as a bubbling noise told her the kettle was boiling. 'How very apt!'

Tane was the Maori word for man, *kaha* for strong. Ian Matheson was a strong man, but his brother-in-law was out on his own.

'And whoever chose his first name must have known what sort of baby they were dealing with,' she decided, pouring the water into the pot. 'Curt by name and curt by nature.'

Grimly amused, she returned to the bookshelves and found another elderly volume. '"English and Scottish Surnames",' she murmured as she flipped through it. '"McIntosh—son of the chieftain"! Somehow I'm not in the least surprised!'

In the chilly bedroom she'd converted into an office, she pulled out a file and sank down at the desk, poring over the lease agreement in search of loopholes.

Curt glanced around his room. The old homestead, now the head shepherd's house, had been transported to another site on the station. In its place Gillian had spent the last two years—and a lot of money—supervising the building of the new house, and then decorating it. Her innate artistry meant that each exquisite room breathed good taste, but she'd paid only lip-service to the homestead's main function as the administrative head of a substantial pastoral concern.

At least she'd kept the integrity of its rural setting and hadn't gone for stark minimalism, he thought drily.

He scanned the photograph on the chest of drawers, taken on the day Gillian married Ian. His sister glowed, so radiantly happy she seemed incandescent with it, and

Ian was smiling down at her, his expression a betraying mixture of tenderness and desire.

Almost the same expression with which he'd looked at Peta Grey in those damned photographs.

What the hell had gone wrong?

It was a rhetorical question. Several things had gone wrong; an urbanite born and bred and a talented artist, Gillian had found it difficult to adjust to life in the country as Ian had worked his way up to managing the biggest station in what Gillian referred to as 'Curt's collection'. She'd stopped painting a couple of years previously, about the time she'd discovered she couldn't have children.

A disappointment Ian clearly shared, Curt thought sternly.

Gillian's suspicions were probably right. In the woman next door, Ian had seen the things his wife lacked—the promise of children and an affinity for the land.

As well, he'd seen something Gillian had missed entirely—a tempting sensuality. Curt swore beneath his breath. Ian's wandering eyes were no longer so startling. Barely concealed beneath the layer of mud and her suspicious antagonism, Peta Grey radiated a vibrant, vital heat that had stirred a dangerous hunger into uncomfortable and reckless life.

It still prowled his body. Not that she was beautiful; *striking* described her exactly. Her skin, fine-grained as the sleekest silk, glowed in the sunlight, its golden tinge echoed by an astonishing golden tracery across her green eyes. Tall and strong, when she walked her lean-limbed, supple grace was like watching music materialise.

Perhaps it was simply her colouring that had got to him; all that gold, he thought with a mocking twist to his smile. Skin, eyes—even the tips of her lashes were gold.

Not to forget the golden-brown hair, thick and glossy as a stream of dark honey.

His brain, not normally given to flights of fancy, summoned from some hidden recess a picture of that hair falling across his chest in silken disorder, and his breath quickened.

Hell! He strode across the room to the desk, stopping to flick up the screen of his laptop. While the state-of-the-art equipment purred into life, he sat down and prepared to concentrate on the task ahead.

But work, which usually took precedence over everything else, didn't do the trick today. When he found himself doodling a pair of sultry eyes and remembering the exact texture of her skin beneath his knuckles as he'd hauled her back from the swamp, and the tantalising pressure of her full breasts against his forearm, he swore again, more luridly this time. After putting down the pen with more than normal care, he crumpled the sheet of paper into a ball and lobbed it into the waste-paper basket with barely concealed violence.

Other women had made an impact on him, but none of them had taken up residence in his mind. He resented that sort of power being wielded by a simple country hick on the make, someone he neither knew nor trusted.

He got to his feet. He was, he realised contemptuously, aroused and unable to control it.

The word 'jealousy' floated across his consciousness, only to be instantly dismissed. There had to be some sort of connection for jealousy to happen.

'Accept it,' he said with cool distaste. 'You want Peta Grey—reluctantly—but you're not going to take up Gillian's suggestion and make a play for her.' His main concern was to get her out of his sister's life, and that process had already begun.

Relieved by the summons of his mobile telephone, he caught it up. His frown wasn't reflected in his voice when he answered the query on the other end. 'Working, but you knew that.'

His lover said something teasing, and he laughed. As Anna spoke he noted the long line of dark trees on the northern horizon. They hid, he knew, the small cottage where Peta Grey lived.

Anna's seductive voice seemed to fade; he had to force himself to concentrate on her conversation, and found it difficult to look away from that row of trees.

'...so I'll see you next Friday night?' Anna asked.

'Yes.'

She knew better than to keep him talking; he hung up with a frown.

Time to put an end to their affair. Anna was trying subtly to work her way into his life, and although their relationship was based on more than sex it would be cruel to let her cherish any false illusions. She wasn't in love with him, but in him she probably saw an excellent chance to establish herself.

As Peta no doubt saw Ian.

His expression hardened. It was time Peta Grey learned that actions always had repercussions.

A knock brought his head up. 'Come in.'

Gillian peered around the door, a gallant smile hiding her tension. 'Lunch in fifteen minutes.'

He nodded. 'I'll be there.'

Once she'd closed the door he glanced at his watch before dialling his lawyers in Auckland.

Peta scanned the cloudless sky, then walked back inside. It was going to be a hot, dry summer and autumn; she could feel it in her bones. Each morning she woke to heat and walked across dewless grass that was slowly fading from green to gold. The springs were already failing, the creeks dwindling. The wind stayed serenely in the north-west, pushing humid air from the tropics over the narrow peninsula that was Northland. In the afternoons taunting clouds built in the sky, huge masses of purple-black and grey, only to disappear over the horizon without following through on their promise.

If no rain came she'd need money for supplemental feed for the calves—money she didn't have, and wouldn't get from the bank.

Moving mechanically, she picked up her lunch dishes and washed them. She just had time to shift the older calves into another paddock, then she'd drive to Kowhai Bay for her stint at the petrol station. Once there she'd ask Sandy if she could work longer hours.

That morning the mail had brought a letter from an Auckland firm of solicitors telling her that it was possible the lease would not be renewed. However the contract to raise calves for Tanekaha Station's dairy herds would remain in effect, although if she decided to sell her farm some agreement could be made in which she wouldn't come out the loser.

The cold, impersonal prose removed any lingering hope that Curt Blackwell McIntosh might change his autocratic mind.

Last night she'd sat over the figures until too late, juggling them as she tried—and failed—to find ways of increasing her income.

And when she'd finally gone to bed she couldn't sleep; instead she lay in bed listening to the familiar night sounds and wondered how much her land would be worth if she put it on the market.

In Kowhai Bay's only petrol station, Sandy shook his head when she asked about more work. 'Sorry, Peta, but it's just not there,' he said, dark eyes sympathetic. 'If I give you extra hours, I'll have to sack someone else.'

'It's OK,' she said quickly. 'Don't worry about it.' But her stomach dropped and the flick of fear beneath her heart strengthened into something perilously like panic.

Her shift over, she called into the only real-estate agency in Kowhai Bay, and asked about the value of her land.

'Not much, I'm afraid—although I'd need to come out and check the house and buildings over.' A year or so older than she was, the agent smiled sympathetically at her as she picked up a volume of district maps, flipping the pages until she found the page she wanted.

Pride stung, Peta held her head high.

'It's a difficult one,' the agent said simply. 'No access, that's the biggie—really, you depend on Tanekaha Station's goodwill to get in and out. I wonder what on earth they were thinking of when they let the previous owners cut that block off the station and sell it to your father.'

'There's an access agreement,' Peta told her.

She didn't look convinced. 'Yes, well, there are other problems too—livestock isn't sexy at the moment, and with last month's trade talks failing, beef prices won't rise for at least a couple of years. Anyway, you don't have enough land to make an income from farming. If you planted olives on it, or avocados, you might attract the lifestyle crowd, but it's too far out of town for most of them. They usually prefer to live close to a beach or on the outskirts. And let's face it, Kowhai Bay hasn't yet reached fashionable status.'

'I hope it never does,' Peta said staunchly.

The agent grinned. 'Come on now, Peta, admit that the place could do with a bit of livening up! For a while after Curt McIntosh bought Tanekaha I thought it might happen, but I suppose it's just too far from Auckland—OK if you're rich enough to fly in and out, but not for anyone else.' She looked up. 'If you're thinking of moving, the logical thing to do is ask McIntosh to buy your block.'

CHAPTER TWO

LOOKED at objectively, the land agent's advice was practical—more or less exactly what Peta had been expecting. But how much would Curt pay for her few hectares? As little as possible, she thought, rubbing the back of her neck in frustration; after all, he held all the cards.

'How much do you think it's worth?' she asked, and sucked in her breath as the woman shrugged.

'You'd need to get it valued properly, but off the top of my head and without prejudice, no more than government valuation.'

'I see.' If it sold for government valuation she'd be able to pay off the mortgage she'd inherited from her father. Nothing more; she'd be adrift with no education, and no skills beyond farming.

Peta left the real-estate office so deep in thought that she almost bumped into someone examining the window of Kowhai Bay's sole boutique.

'Peta!'

'Oh—Nadine!' Laughing, they embraced. Peta stepped back and said admiringly, 'Aren't you the fine up-and-coming city lawyer! I guessed you'd be home for Granny Wai's ninetieth birthday.'

'Absolutely. She's so looking forward to it, you can't imagine!'

That night Peta saw for herself. The big hall at the local marae was crowded with people, many of them the matriarch's descendants, mingling with neighbours, local dignitaries, and visitors from points around the world.

36

Surrounded by flowers and streamers and balloons, relishing the laughter and the gossip and the reunions, Granny held court in an elegant black dress, heirloom greenstone *hei-tiki* pendant gleaming on her breast.

Nadine pushed politely past a couple of elderly men to say with envy, 'That honey-gold colour suits you superbly. Did you make your top?'

'Yes.' Peta enjoyed sewing, and the silky, sleeveless garment had only taken a couple of hours to finish.

'Thought so.' She turned and waved to her great-grandmother. 'Isn't she amazing? You watch—as soon as the band strikes up she'll be on the floor. Pino's threatened to jive with her, and Mum's terrified she'll break her hip, but if Granny wants to jive, Granny will! She's as tough as old boots, bless her.'

A subdued stir by the door caught their attention.

'Uh-oh,' Nadine said beneath her breath. 'Speaking of tough, the Tanekaha Station clan has just arrived.'

Peta opened her mouth then closed it again. Of course the Mathesons and Curt would have been invited.

Her friend sighed elaborately. 'You know, Curt McIntosh is a magnificent, gorgeous man. Pity he's got the soul of a shark.'

'A shark?' Jolted, Peta glanced across the room, in time to see Curt lift Granny's hand to his mouth and kiss it.

The gesture should have looked stagy and incongruous, but he carried it off with a panache that sent heat shafting down her spine. Dragging her gaze back to Nadine's face, she asked, 'A shark as in being dishonest and sleazy?'

'Oh, no, never that! He's got a reputation for absolute

fairness; deal well with him, and he'll deal well with you. Just don't expect any loving kindness,' her friend said drily. 'Of course, sharks can't help being the most lethal predators in the sea. It's inborn in them, like being cold-blooded and dangerous.' She peered across the intervening crowd. 'I thought he might bring along the latest very good friend, Anna Lee, but clearly no. This wouldn't be her scene, anyway.'

'Hmm, I deduce that you know her and don't like her.' Peta refused to wonder why discovering that Curt had a lover seared into her composure as painfully as an acid burn.

Her friend rolled her eyes. 'I saw them together a couple of nights ago at her art exhibition. She is very chic. She is very artistic. She does installations. And she thinks lawyers—especially those who haven't yet clawed their way off the bottom rung—are Philistine scum.'

Laughing, Peta shot another glance across the hall, something inside her twisting as her eyes were captured by an enigmatic grey-blue gaze. Curt McIntosh's dark head inclined in a nod that had something regal to it.

Not to be outdone, she responded with an aloof smile before turning back to Nadine. 'Don't tell me you *told* her you didn't like her installations?'

'Of course not!' Nadine primmed her mouth. 'I have much better manners than that. My expression must have given me away. But when I buy an installation it will be more substantial than a collection of found objects depicting the primordial rhythm of creation.'

Peta grinned. 'Urk!'

'Just so,' Nadine said smugly. 'But she's very beautiful, so I don't blame the fabulous Curt for falling for her, even though I'd have expected more from him. He's completely brilliant.' She sighed and added with a smirk,

'It's a pity men are such superficial beings. Yet they've got the gall to claim that *we're* driven by hormones!'

It was almost impossible to imagine Curt at the mercy of his hormones, Peta decided. He might behave like a shark, but he was fully in control.

On the other hand what did she know about the other sex? Nothing much, just enough to be certain that she was never going to marry a dominant man. Her father's rigid insistence on being head of the family had been enough for her; when—if—she married, she'd choose a kind, decent man who understood that women had needs and brains and the right to have an opinion.

'Evolution has a lot to answer for,' she said brightly, and for the next half-hour or so managed to ignore Curt and the Mathesons.

Later, after several dances and an animated conversation with another school friend who'd come back from Australia for the occasion, she turned around, tossing a laughing remark over her shoulder as she headed off to pay her respects to Granny.

Only to discover a large male blocking her path; she pulled up in mid-stride, stopping far too close to a faultless white shirt and a magnificently tailored suit.

Before she had time to draw breath two strong hands gripped her upper arms. Heat radiated through her in a wild, impulsive flood as Curt murmured in a deep, sardonic voice for her ears only, 'I seem to be making a habit of this.'

He released her, but didn't move away. Around them people talked and laughed and called out, yet she was trapped with him in sizzling silence.

Peta thought headily that the air between them must be glittering in a frenzy of electrons and atoms, or whatever it was made of. She almost looked down to check whether tiny lightning flashes connected them in fierce, strange intimacy.

Pasting a smile onto trembling lips, she mustered her defences and said, 'Be grateful—there's no mud this time.'

Mockery gleamed between his dense black lashes. 'A complete change of appearance,' he agreed with a disturbing intonation that sent more hot little shivers down her spine.

He didn't move; she couldn't. His will and determination bored into her like some psychic energy.

And although she knew it was dangerous, that she should step back, make some light, stupid remark and *get the hell out of there*, she lifted her head and looked him in the face. He was smiling, yet something formidable about his expression reminded her sharply of Nadine's words, although his eyes challenged her description of him as a shark, because sharks were inhumanly cold.

Whereas heat burned in Curt's eyes and touched his smile with a tantalising promise of passionate satisfaction. It enveloped her—a potent, charged aura of sexual charisma hot enough to set sirens clamouring in every cell of her body. Shocked and bewildered, she felt her breasts expand and an odd, drawing sensation tighten their peaks, both disconcerting and intensely pleasurable.

If she didn't get out of there he'd see what was happening. Panicking, she dragged air into her lungs, feeding enough oxygen to her starved brain to prod her instincts into life.

She stepped away and thankfully fell back on the inanities of polite small talk. 'Hello, Curt. Fancy seeing you here.' She hoped that he hadn't heard the feverish inflection in each word.

Fat chance.

His eyes glinted and his smile hardened into mockery. 'Why the surprise?' he drawled.

'It doesn't seem quite your sort of thing.' Desperate to get away, she glanced at her watch. 'I'm just on my way to wish the guest of honour a happy birthday, so if you'll excuse—'

A flourish of chords from the band broke into her words, silencing the chatter; when it died one of Granny's great-grandsons seized the microphone and announced, 'A special request from Granny—an invitation waltz!'

The youngsters groaned, but when Granny chose one of them to dance, the teenager partnered her with expert ease.

'I don't think she's interested in talking to you just now,' Curt said satirically.

'I realise that.' The tension and fear that had ridden her since he'd informed her of his cold-blooded decision to not renew the lease had returned, almost replacing that fierce, perilous awareness. How on earth was she to get away from him without making herself look a fool?

And then the music stopped, and Granny appeared in front of them, her autocratic face alight with humour as she chose Curt.

'Stay there,' she commanded Peta. 'I'll send him back to you when I've finished with him.'

Everyone around laughed, including Peta, although she felt as though her hostess's teasing words had branded her. Once the band started up again, she seized the opportunity to disappear into the crowd, but before she'd taken more than a couple of steps she was claimed by one of Nadine's cousins for the waltz.

They barely had time to catch up on their lives before the young master of ceremonies called out, 'Change again, everyone, for the last time!' and her partner whirled her back to the place he'd found her.

And to Curt.

'Here she is, man,' her partner said, grinning as he relinquished her. 'Apart from Granny she's the best dancer in the room.'

Curt said something Peta didn't catch, but it made Nadine's cousin laugh.

'My dance,' Curt said, and there was nothing humorous in his tone.

Peta stiffened, but she couldn't refuse to dance with him. Heady anticipation battling pride, she let herself be turned into his embrace and swept onto the floor.

Big men were often a little awkward, but not Curt; he moved with a smooth grace that had a strangely weakening effect on her spine and knees. Although the arm around her waist kept her a fraction of an inch away from him, she was sharply, painfully aware of a faint scent, warm and male and sexy, that owed nothing to aftershave.

The melting sensation in the pit of her stomach transmuted into a flood of terrifying response that came too close to hunger. She didn't *do* instant attraction—but then she'd never met another man with this combination of authority and sexual confidence.

'I've met your stunning friend before,' he said. 'In Auckland at an art exhibition.'

'Yes, she told me. You were with the artist.'

Before he could answer an elderly couple strayed into their path. Curt swung her around, pulling her closer as they moved smoothly into a pivot that carried them out of the way of the other dancers.

For a couple of seconds she lay against him, one

heavily muscled leg between hers as he turned her, his arm hard across her back. A hot pulse of forbidden pleasure throbbed along her veins and her brain shut down, allowing every tiny stimulus to run riot through her.

And then his arm loosened. For a second she was so dazzled by his closeness that she stayed where she was, until she caught the nearest dancers exchanging knowing smiles.

Abruptly she pulled away. Curt looked down at her, eyes gleaming blue fire beneath his thick lashes. He knew his effect on her.

Sick humiliation ate into her. She stared blindly over his shoulder at the whirling, blurring mass of dancers.

'Anna Lee,' he said.

'What?'

His voice hardened. 'The artist.'

'Oh. Yes, I see.' Pride tightened her sinews, gave her the composure to say evenly, 'Nadine told me that she does installations.'

She was acting like a half-wit, but it was the best reply she could force from a brain that had crumbled into sawdust.

'She does indeed.' The note of irony in his words scraped along her nerves. 'How's the calf?'

Peta marshalled her thoughts into ragged order. 'She seems fine,' she said, trying hard to sound composed and in control.

He swung her around again, and she felt his upper arm flex beneath her fingers. Something hot and feral sizzled through her like fire in dry grass, blazing into swift life.

Surely the music had lasted far longer in this set than any other?

Just then to her intense relief it stopped, and the DJ

called out, 'OK, ten minutes for talking, and then we start again!'

Curt McIntosh looked down at her, blue eyes hooded, handsome face impassive. 'Thank you,' he said formally.

Peta produced a smile. 'It was lovely,' she lied. 'Oh, Nadine's waving to me! I'll see what she wants.'

She gave him another smile, a little more genuine this time, and escaped, intent on getting away before her precarious self-possession evaporated entirely.

For the rest of the evening Curt didn't come near her again. On her way home in the small hours she told herself vigorously that she was glad. Dancing with him had been like dancing with temptation...

'And I don't do temptation either,' she told herself as she unlocked her front door.

But before she escaped into the silent house she stooped and picked a gardenia flower from the bush by the steps. Its sweet, sinfully evocative scent floated through her bedroom as she lay awake and fought a treacherous need to retrace every moment she'd spent in Curt's arms.

She stared into the darkness, seeing again the glinting irony in his gaze when he'd realised that her body responded helplessly to the heat and strength of his.

'Stop it,' she commanded herself. 'He was having fun with you, and it wasn't kind. Sharks are predators, and this one wants to take you out of circulation.'

How long was he going to stay at Tanekaha? For a while she toyed with the idea of ringing Gillian Matheson and saying she couldn't come to the barbecue the following night; she could manufacture an emergency easily enough.

But that would be cowardice.

So she'd go. She'd cope because she had to. She

wasn't going to give Curt the chance to laugh at her
again.

Shaken by a sudden ache of longing for something she
didn't understand, she turned over, curled her long body
in the bed and wooed sleep with such fervour that eventually she achieved it.

Peta heard the sound of the engine just before breakfast.
Frowning, she closed the gate behind her and turned to
see the station Land Rover come up the drive. Her heart
jumped unexpectedly, only to go cold when Ian's rangy
form unfolded from behind the wheel.

'Hello,' she said warily.

'How are you?'

Ever since she'd noticed the worrying change in his
attitude she'd braced herself for this meeting. Without
moving, she said brightly, 'I'm fine, thanks. What can I
do for you?'

'You could make me a cup of coffee,' he suggested
with a wry smile.

Ten days ago she wouldn't have thought a thing about
it; she'd have made the coffee and they'd have drunk it
sitting on the narrow deck while they talked easily about
farming matters.

'I'd love to,' she said easily, 'but I'm on my way to
feed a calf your brother-in-law helped me drag out of the
swamp.'

'I'll come with you.'

After a moment's hesitation she turned and led the way
to the calf-shed.

Hiding her wary discomfort with a brisk veneer, she
made up the mixture and stayed to make sure the calf
drank it. 'She must be feeling better; this time yesterday
she didn't want to drink at all.'

Ian observed, 'Curt told us about it.'

'I'd have managed without him,' she said quickly, sad because the friendship and support Ian had offered so unstintingly was shattered. He'd stepped over an invisible boundary and now there was no going back.

He said casually, 'It looks pretty good now.'

'She'll survive.'

Ian's face crinkled into a wry smile. 'Good. What did you think of Curt?'

Peta made a production of her shrug. 'He's more or less as I'd imagined him.'

Ian said, 'And that is?'

'Like any other tycoon,' she said lightly. 'Dominating, formidable, high-handed and more than a bit arrogant.'

He nodded and got to his feet. 'Good-looking too.'

'Yes.' But Curt's handsome face and the impact of his strong bone structure were irrelevant. Like a force of nature, his compelling personality overwhelmed everything else.

Her upwards glance caught an unusual indecision in Ian's face, as though he was trying to make up his mind about something.

Suspecting that it would be better if he never said the words that were in his mind, she said, 'Shouldn't you be on your way home? Gillian will be wondering where you are.'

'Gillian isn't—' The noise of a car engine coming up the drive stopped him in mid-sentence. He turned his head so that he could see through the open end of the shed and in a flat voice said, 'This is her car.'

Peta froze. She hated scenes, and she suspected she was about to be treated to one. Ian moved jerkily out into the sunlight, but she sat there watching the calf drink, ears straining as the engine cut out.

Voices revealed that it was Gillian who'd driven up. And with her, Curt.

Peta's skin tightened as she took in the pattern of sounds, of silences. She should get up and go out; instead, she kept her eyes fixed on the white brush at the end of the calf's tail, watching it swish to and fro as the little animal sucked.

When she heard Gillian's laugh she relaxed a fraction, only to tense up again as the voices approached. Above the calf's noisy, enthusiastic slurps she heard Curt's deep voice, and the foreboding that had been prowling below the surface of her consciousness since the previous night rocketed off the scale.

'Hello, Peta,' Gillian called out. 'Can we come in?'

'Of course.' Still she kept her eyes on the calf, only looking up when it became rude not to acknowledge them.

Clad in casual clothes that proclaimed the imprint of a designer, Gillian looked completely out of place in the calf-shed with its dusty smell of hay and the more earthy scent of young animals. His expression a combination of stubbornness and indecision, Ian walked behind his wife.

In fact, Peta realised, the only person whose self-assurance remained intact and invulnerable was Curt.

Wondering if anything ever put a crack in his self-assurance, Peta greeted them with a brief smile. 'Have you come to examine the patient? As you can see, she's in good heart today.'

Gillian made a soft clucking noise. 'What a pretty little thing,' she cooed, and leaned over to give the curly poll a scratch. 'I thought she'd be covered in mud!'

'No, I brushed her down and dried her yesterday.'

'You didn't explain how she got into the swamp.'

Curt's voice, anger running beneath each deliberate word like lava welling through rocks.

The hairs on the back of Peta's neck stood on end in primitive reaction. 'I don't know what spooked her into the swamp, but she was well and truly stuck when I found her.' She smiled wryly. 'And when Curt rode up on his big black horse Laddie's impersonation of a werewolf in hysterics didn't help—the calf bolted even further into the mud.'

Laddie apparently considered the sound of his name to be an invitation and ran towards the calf-pen just as the little animal turned to survey its audience.

'Get in behind!' Peta commanded sternly, leaping up from the hay bale to grab his collar. Her foot slid over a stone and turned her ankle. Although she regained her balance instantly, Ian grabbed her arm.

When Peta said the first thing that came to her mind, it was in a thin voice she hardly recognised. 'Thank you, Ian, but it was just a stone.'

He dropped his hand. 'I thought you were going to end up on your nose!'

Peta prayed no one would recognise the artificial timbre of her laugh. 'That would be twice in twenty-four hours. Curt had to drag me out of the swamp yesterday.'

Curt said, 'Gillian, why don't you go home with Ian? I have something to discuss with Peta. I'll bring your car back, and I won't be more than ten minutes or so.'

The words fell into a silence echoing with repressed emotions. His sister broke it by saying brightly, 'Make sure it's no more than ten minutes; *you* know Mrs Harkness gets very tense when we're late for meals, and *I* know how easily you get sidetracked when business calls.' Her smile at Peta lacked warmth as she linked her arm in her husband's. 'Come on, darling. Take me home.'

His gaze fixed on Curt, Ian said, 'I'll see you when you get back.'

Curt's brows lifted, but he waited until they'd driven away before turning to Peta, still frozen with dismay. She swallowed and met his gaze, hard as flint. Defensively, she folded her arms across her chest and lifted her chin.

In a level voice that didn't conceal the iron in his words, he said, 'If you carry on this thing with Ian you'll regret it.'

He knew. How? Surely that quick grip of Ian's hand hadn't given away his secret? Peta knew she looked guilty and she knew it was unfair—she had done absolutely nothing to precipitate Ian's infatuation.

Without waiting for an answer Curt went on, 'Because cutting off the lease will be only the first step to taking everything you've got away from you.'

Starkly conscious of the ruthless determination in his tone, Peta blurted, 'There is no *thing* with Ian.'

'Don't lie to me.'

'I'm not lying,' she said aggressively, heart thudding crazily beneath her crossed arms. 'And I'm not scared of empty threats. There's no way you can do that.'

'I'll make your life here impossible,' he returned with cold precision. 'To start off with, I'll deny you access over Tanekaha land.'

She stared at him, her swift response drying on her lips. He couldn't do that. Yet one glance from those flat, lethal eyes and Peta knew he would. 'My father had an agreement—'

'It isn't worth the paper it's written on. Any halfway decent lawyer would have it thrown out of court. And if you don't believe me, I'll pay for you to have an independent opinion,' he said contemptuously. He waited for the implications of this to sink in before adding with a brutal lack of emotion, 'Without access your land is valueless—worth only what I'd be prepared to pay for it. And if you run off with Ian that will be peanuts.'

He meant it. Suddenly scared, Peta said harshly, 'I don't plan to run off with him. I don't want—'

'I don't care what *you* want. He wants you—that's obvious. Are you sleeping with him?'

'No!'

Her voice vibrated with outrage, but Curt knew how easy it was to assume that offended tone. One of his lovers had given a very convincing display when he'd told her that he refused to share her sexual favours. He'd had proof then too.

He shrugged. 'Not that it matters. But if you believe that breaking up Ian's marriage will get you a better life, you're wrong. He won't only lose his wife, he'll be out of a job and I'll make sure he never works as anything more than a farmhand for the rest of his life. You might be happy with that; trust me, Ian won't be.'

Green fire mixed with gold flamed in her eyes. Heat radiated from her, enriching the golden lights in her hair and the smooth, warm silk of her skin. Curt resisted the hard pull of lust in his groin.

'I don't want to break up *any* marriage,' she said fiercely, uncrossing her arms to place a hand firmly on each hip. 'Ian means nothing to me.'

So she was just using the poor bastard. Anger gave Curt's words formidable intensity. 'But what do you mean to him?'

Her white teeth bit into her full lower lip. Curt's blood surged through his veins; she managed to invest the most trivial of gestures with an innate sensuality that damned near splintered his self-control.

Face set, she expanded, 'I don't know, and I don't care! He's always been a kind of father figure—for heaven's sake, he must be twenty years older than I am!'

'Twelve. What's that got to do with anything?'

Peta had never disliked anyone so much as she disliked him, a dislike bolstered by a cold, crawling fear. He had every intention of forcing her out of his sister's life—she only had to look at his ruthless face to know that she didn't have a chance of changing his mind.

Panic made her reckless. 'I'm not in the habit of having affairs with men twelve years older than I am!'

One raised brow told her what he thought of that. 'In that case, we might be able to save the situation.'

The calf shuffled about in the hay, the soft noise knotting her nerves.

'What do you mean?' she asked, hating this surrender even though she wanted nothing more than to get out of this uncomfortable situation.

'It's quite simple.'

She held her breath as he finished, 'All you have to do is make it obvious you don't want anything he's offering.'

She clenched her teeth, but however crude his words were, he'd only put into words the decision she'd already made. 'I'll tell him.'

Curt shook his head. 'You'll show him,' he said succinctly.

Startled, she looked up into a face set in lines as ruthless as any pagan warrior. 'How?'

'You'll transfer your affections to me,' he told her silkily.

His words rang meaninglessly in Peta's ears. 'What?'

CHAPTER THREE

THE colour drained from Peta's skin, leaving her cold and shocked. She couldn't have heard him correctly.

One glance at Curt's implacable face went a long way towards convincing her. He *had* just said, 'You'll transfer your affections to me.'

'No,' she blurted. 'I... You don't have to go that far. I'll just tell him that—that—'

'You'll tell him nothing,' Curt stated imperiously. 'He'll get the message when you start looking sideways at me from beneath your lashes.'

She was shaking. 'No, it's impossible. What about your friend—the artist?'

His face hardened even further. 'Your concern for her welfare does you credit, although I'd believe in it more if you weren't jeopardising my sister's marriage without any apparent qualm.'

'I tell you, I didn't realise—'

He interrupted with a coldly determined, 'I'm not interested in what you knew or realised, or even whether you set a honey trap for Ian. It's not relevant. And neither is my relationship with Anna.'

For some reason this blunt statement cut deeply. Peta flashed, 'Or only in so far as it makes me look like a woman on the make, one who doesn't care who she hurts.'

'Exactly. Concentrate on convincing Ian that you took one look at me and decided to go for the big money.'

Curt's smile was a masterpiece of cold cynicism. 'No man likes to be played for a fool by a gold-digger.'

Bewildered, she thought that he shouldn't be able to wound her with such accurate, painful precision. Normally she gave as good as she got; after that insult she had to drag in a painful breath before persisting stubbornly, 'It won't work. I mean—' she gestured at herself '—we don't have anything in common. Ian won't believe it.'

He gave a short, surprised laugh. 'You're not my usual type,' he agreed suavely, 'but Ian's a man, and what you're offering is pretty obvious. He'll be jealous, but he won't be surprised if I take you up on it.'

Enraged, Peta said, 'You—you arrogant bastard!'

'But rich,' he returned with silky derision. 'And for Ian, that's all that's going to matter. As for your clothes, I can fix that.'

Instant suspicion darkened her eyes. 'How?' If he thought she was going into debt at Kowhai Bay's boutique for clothes she'd never wear again, he had another think coming.

'A quick trip to Auckland will provide you with a suitable wardrobe to enhance your not inconsiderable assets.'

Although his deliberate tone chilled her and his hard blue-grey gaze remained fixed on her face, she knew that he'd catalogued every one of those assets. Shamed by a furtive tingle of arousal, she stiffened her shoulders. 'I can't afford a make over.'

'I shall, of course, pay.'

A niggle of pain throbbed in Peta's temple, but she met his eyes without flinching. 'You won't, because I won't do it. The whole idea is impossible—ridiculous.' In her steadiest voice she added the clincher. 'We don't even like each other.'

His brows rose. 'Liking,' he said indifferently, 'has nothing to do with this sort of relationship.'

Peta shook her head. Although she had her pick of scathing observations, spitting any of them out would reveal how much his high-handed attitude hurt her, so she took refuge in silence.

Curt waited, then finished, 'And after seeing us dance together at the marae no one will be surprised.'

Humiliated pride slashed her composure to shreds. Some hidden part of her had been cherishing the memory of that dance with its reckless undercurrent of carnality. Had he been planning this then?

Of course he had, she thought furiously. Nadine was right; he was as cold-blooded as a shark.

Curt waited until it was obvious she wasn't going to answer before finishing, 'So I'll pick you up tonight.'

'Tonight—oh, the barbecue.' Head held high, she met his eyes defiantly. 'I'm not going.'

Although not a muscle in the big, lithe body moved, Peta's senses reacted instantly to an unspoken threat. Adrenalin poured through her and she took an involuntary step backwards. Every sense alert, she forced herself to stand her ground, to meet ice-cold eyes and drag in a deep breath.

The world went still. Into a silence so intense she felt it on her skin like a hammer, he said lethally, 'I don't hurt women.'

'I don't know that.' Her heart pounded as though she'd run a marathon, but beneath the fear burned a bewildering exhilaration. For the first time he was looking at her as a person, not as a woman to be manipulated. And he didn't like her fear.

'You know it now.' His lips barely moved.

Eyes huge in her face, she steeled herself to say, 'I

have only your word for it. Why should I believe you when you don't believe me?'

'Believe it.'

She stared at him, then slowly nodded. 'For some strange reason,' she admitted, 'I do. But just in case I'm wrong, you believe that I don't like being threatened.'

Curt shrugged, but colour along his warrior's cheekbones belied his controlled tone. 'You say you don't want Ian to fall in love with you. A relationship between us will kill his affection faster than anything else. Yes, you'll look like a woman on the make. That, surely, is a small price to pay.'

It made cold, hard sense. After all, what did she have to lose? Only her pride. She bit her lip and said resentfully, 'All right. Except that this is a fake relationship.'

'Of course,' he said contemptuously. 'Think of this whole business as a sharp warning to keep your eyes off married men in the future.'

The unfairness of the accusation stung. 'I didn't—'

'I saw a photograph of the two of you together,' he interrupted, his tone scathing. 'Ian's hand was touching your cheek in what was definitely a caress. And you weren't saying no.'

The memory of the pigeon, spooked by something in the plum tree, flashed across Peta's mind. 'Who took it?' she demanded. Surely not Gillian?

'A visiting kid with a new digital camera was trying to get a photograph of the bird. Instead, she got that photo, followed by one of the bird as it flew out of the tree. By then you were both looking at the camera.'

Peta swallowed. 'If she'd waited a second longer she'd have got a photograph of me leaving in haste. And I've made sure I haven't seen him alone since then.'

One black brow lifted in ironic disbelief. 'Until this morning,' he drawled.

Clearly, he was never going to give her even the slightest benefit of the doubt—for him, there was no doubt. He was arrogantly convinced she'd decided to go after Ian and in pursuit of her own advantage, to hell with Gillian's happiness or anything else.

She said desperately, 'Curt, this won't work. It takes more than acting to fool people.'

'Acting?'

Intuition told her what was going to happen next. Run! a despairing inner voice commanded, but an even older instinct locked her muscles so that when he pulled her into his arms she made no attempt to escape the inevitable.

'I don't think we'll need to act,' he said smoothly, and bent his head and kissed her.

It was a blatant act of mastery, possessive and angry, yet when Peta tried to resist, her body refused to accept the commands of her brain. Any other man who crowded her like this would have taken a fist in the solar plexus followed by a knee to his most sensitive region. Instead, treacherous desire and a fierce curiosity kept her prisoner until his kiss worked a barbaric enchantment.

A low sound in her throat startled her; her mouth softened beneath the demanding insistence of his, and an overwhelming tide of passion hit her, so fiercely elemental that it shocked her into surrender.

She had no idea how much later Curt lifted his head. Hugely reluctant, she opened her eyes, flinching when the glitter in his was replaced by a taunt.

'I don't think either of us will have to do much acting,' he said with cool confidence as he let her go.

Mortified, Peta realised she was clutching his shirt. She

jerked free of the pressure of his big, aroused body, shivering in the breeze that flowed over acutely sensitised skin.

She'd given him a potent weapon, she realised, infuriated and humiliated by the amused satisfaction in his expression. Rashly, she stated, 'That was assault.'

His eyes gleamed and he gave her a slow, mocking smile. 'Only if you didn't want it.'

Hot-cheeked and indignant, Peta opened her mouth to refute this, but he said brusquely, 'Don't muddy the waters. You wanted it—you couldn't have made it plainer. And you turned to fire when we kissed.'

Throat aching from unspoken tension, she said hoarsely, 'Don't ever do it again.'

He shrugged indolently. 'You're going to have to get used to it, because Ian won't believe in a platonic relationship. If we're going to convince Ian that you've latched on to a better prospect, you'll need to be physically aware of me.'

His brutal bluntness told her how much he despised her. It slashed like a stockwhip across her skin, but she ignored it. He could well be right, she thought wearily. Ian had his pride; he wouldn't want his brother-in-law's leftovers. 'Are you sure this will work?'

'It had better.'

The cold note of menace in his tone tightened every nerve. 'And if it doesn't?'

'Then you'll lose your farm,' he said pleasantly. 'And in case you get any ideas, don't think he'll be able to help you. In New Zealand law, half of what he owns goes to Gillian.'

When she frowned he said in a tone that lifted the hairs on the back of her neck, 'Didn't he tell you that Gillian's money is held in trust for her? If they divorce he'll have nothing; certainly not enough to buy any land.'

Because he was the trustee, she'd bet.

But he had a few good points; he helped her get the calf out of the swamp, and he had to love his sister to be prepared to go slumming for her...

He watched her face, and after a taut few seconds added deliberately, 'Don't worry, you won't lose financially by joining me in this masquerade.'

Dominating swine, tarring everyone with his own brush! Green-gold eyes glittering, she asked sweetly, 'Does money solve everything for you?'

'Most things,' he said, sounding amused. 'Don't knock it. And if you want to find out how important it is, tell Ian about this.'

With gritty emphasis she said, 'You needn't worry— I'll pretend as well as I can.' She flicked a lock of hair back from her hot face and finished fiercely, 'You're lucky you have a ready-made way to force me into it. What would you have done if you didn't have the power to deny me road access?'

'I'd have offered you more money, of course,' he said coolly. 'I assume you see him as a source of security, and although paying you off goes against the grain, I can provide you with more than he ever could.'

Her lip curled. 'I'm not for sale.'

He laughed beneath his breath and reached for her, linking his fingers at the back of her neck with exquisite gentleness before using his thumbs to force up her chin. 'Everyone's for sale,' he said quietly. 'All a buyer has to do is find the right price.'

'So what would it take to buy you?' she asked in an odd, stifled voice, driven by a strange combination of fury and compassion.

Eyes narrowed into crystalline slivers, he examined her face. 'More than you can pay,' he said with raw intensity. 'More than you could ever pay.'

And he dropped his hands to pull her into him so that he could kiss her again, taking her mouth with urgent hunger in a kiss driven by a dangerous volatility. His mouth devoured hers—and hers met and matched his hunger. Her treacherous body leapt into full life, blazing with a storm of desire made even more intense by the complex turmoil of her emotions.

Every warning bolted from her brain; only when his hand came up to rest on her breast, and she felt the eager centre tighten against his palm did she realise what she had to do.

She yanked herself back; somehow her hair had become loose and when she shook her head a cloud of golden-brown swirled around her stunned face.

Instantly, as though he'd been waiting, Curt let her go and stood staring at her with a black hostility that tightened every quivering nerve into knots.

Attack first. 'You promised that wouldn't happen again,' she accused.

'It won't,' he said harshly. 'I'll see you later.'

He swung on his heel and left her there in the calfshed with the familiar scents of animals and hay and the milk mixture, and her heart drumming in a dangerous rhythm of anticipation and excitement and anger.

'One day,' she muttered when the car started up outside, 'I hope you fall desperately in love with someone, and I pray she tells you just how bloody-minded and patronising you are and then turns you down *flat*.'

Laddie stretched enthusiastically and yawned, his jaws making a faint clop as they came together.

Peta grimaced and bent to scratch the dog. 'Just as well

you're not a guard dog, or I'd be sending you off to the SPCA for dereliction of duty. Why didn't you sink your teeth into his ankle?'

Her voice shook, and as his tail swept from side to side, her attempted smile turned into a trembling contraction of her mouth. She straightened up. 'OK, we'd better do some work and after that I'll work out exactly what I'm wearing to this wretched barbecue.'

In the end she chose a gold shirt she'd made a couple of years previously, combining it with a pair of cuffed trousers the same bronze as her only decent sandals.

So far, so good. She checked herself out in the mirror, frowning when she caught a glimpse of bra through the thin cotton of her shirt. After a moment's thought she opened a drawer and found a camel-coloured T-shirt and put it on under the shirt.

Yes, that was more discreet, although slightly too warm in the humid heat of Northland. Still, after her utter folly in Curt's arms, discretion came first.

In spite of everything, there was a sly satisfaction in looking good. Mouth set in a smile that held more irony than amusement, she tied her hair back with a fine loop of leather and picked up her lipstick. Its warm peachy toning reinforced the lushness of her tender lips.

She was scared. Already in too deep with Curt McIntosh, she vowed that from now on she'd be cool and composed and completely unavailable.

But when Laddie began barking enthusiastically above the low growl of an engine, an aggressive, heady anticipation hollowed out her stomach. For the last time she checked herself in the mirror, and gaped in startled wonder at the difference. She looked alive—skin glowing, mouth full and sensuous, gold sparks lighting up the green depths of her eyes. Even her hair shimmered with new life and vibrancy.

Curt McIntosh should patent his kisses; they'd make him a fortune in the rejuvenation market!

And people were going to notice, she thought uncomfortably.

'Well, that's the point of this whole farcical charade,' she said aloud in a hard voice.

So she wanted Curt McIntosh. Big deal. As long as she didn't make the cardinal mistake of confusing desire with love, she'd be fine. Passion was less complex and infinitely safer. She'd seen first-hand how love could betray. Her mother had given up everything for it—her family and friends, her talent at music, her health. Worn down by hard work and lack of money, she'd struggled through the years because she'd loved her husband.

And in the end it had killed her.

Peta's jaw firmed. No way was she going to surrender to that. Her independence was too precious to jeopardise by losing her heart.

That thought gave her enough calmness to pick up her small bag and open the front door. Tall and autocratic, the sun coaxing blue-black shadows in his dark head, Curt stepped back and lifted his brows, surveying her with open appreciation. Her stupid stomach performed an acrobatic manoeuvre that left her breathless.

Cool, she commanded. Be very, very cool. Right now.

'Quite a transformation.' He bent to pick a bloom from the gardenia by the steps.

'I assume that's a compliment,' she said in a muted voice, overwhelmed by the sight of him in a casual shirt the same grey-blue as his eyes, and sleek black trousers that hugged his hips and made the most of his long legs.

His blue eyes mocked her. 'Of course.' He tucked the

gardenia into his top buttonhole and waited while she locked the door.

This time he was driving a Range Rover, a massive thing that combined power with restrained luxury. From his kennel, Laddie watched interestedly as Curt opened the passenger door and closed it behind her.

Already belted in by the time he got in behind the wheel, she linked her hands in her lap and thought, *Cool!* He was far too big, and in the confined space he loomed when he turned to examine her, a frown drawing his brows together.

Hiding her dilating eyes with a quick sweep of her lashes, she stared at the fine-grained olive skin of his throat and demanded, 'What is it?'

A swift hand found the leather tie in her hair and pulled it smoothly down over her ponytail.

'Hey!' she spluttered. Her hair swirled free, settling in a thick topaz cloud across her shoulders; she looked down to see a wave of it sift over his wrist. The westering sun burnished it into a flame of gold and cognac. Her heart began to pound in her ears, a cynical little drum informing her that although her mind and her will might want one thing, her body had its own agenda.

He drawled, 'That's much more grown-up,' and dropped the strip of leather into his pocket as he switched on the engine.

'Agreeing to this doesn't give you the right to man-handle me,' she told him tautly.

He gave her a sardonic smile and backed the vehicle skilfully around. 'I promised not to kiss you. Anything else goes. I'll do whatever needs to be done to save my sister's marriage. And in case you didn't know, what you call manhandling is an indication of attraction.'

Peta opened her mouth to speak, then closed her lips again.

'You were going to say?' he enquired as the vehicle swung out onto the road—his road, she thought bitterly.

'I was going to ask if her marriage was worth saving,' she said.

'That's her decision.' He turned his head to flash a brief, white smile at her. 'So do your best tonight, Peta. No flinching girlishly if I touch you, plenty of smiles and lots of play with those astonishing eyelashes.'

Peta had been to several parties at the homestead before—not the A-list ones, of course, just the neighbourhood affairs. Walking beside a silent Curt through the gardens towards a rear terrace, she thought bleakly that he must love his sister very much to initiate this sham relationship. How had he convinced his lover to agree to it? The thought of Anna Lee, artist and snob, rubbed her already raw nerves painfully.

Curt looked at her. 'Smile.'

She produced a wide, false grin. 'Don't expect me to gaze adoringly into your eyes. No one who knows me would believe it.'

'Didn't you gaze adoringly into the eyes of your previous lovers?'

'No,' she said, clipping the word short. There had been no previous lovers, but that was no business of his.

'I expect you to follow my lead in everything I do,' he said softly, and when her eyes flashed he went on with grim emphasis, 'Or else.'

Actually, he played it perfectly. Inherent sophistication meant he didn't make a show of his supposed interest; he staked his claim far more subtly with glances and smiles, the occasional touch of his hand on her waist or arm, and his possessive air. In an odd way it made her feel protected and safe, and that, she thought warily, was even more dangerous than the flash-fire of sexual hunger she felt whenever he touched her.

If it hadn't been for Ian and Gillian she might have enjoyed the evening, but in their presence she felt as though she were teetering on the edge of a perilous cliff, exposed and vulnerable, waiting for someone to push her over.

Born a hostess, Gillian had done an excellent job with the gardens; from the terrace around the swimming pool parents could sip and watch their children swim, and those who felt energetic worked it off at the tennis courts behind high, vine-covered walls. Any who demanded less strenuous activity tried their hand at *petanque*.

The Mathesons were gracious, as charming as they had ever been, yet an hour later Peta looked around the lovely grounds, the laughing people, and wondered why no one else sensed the strain between their hosts.

'You're doing well,' Curt said, bending as though he were murmuring sweet nothings in her ear.

Painfully aware of Ian's swift glance, she froze.

Curt directed a narrow smile at her. He lifted his hand to her chin and commanded, 'Another smile, Peta.'

The sensual force of his masculinity hit her like a shock wave. She met his half-closed, intent stare with eyes grown dark and her breath barely coming through her lips.

'On second thoughts, that's even better,' he said after a pause, his voice suddenly rough.

You're giving too much away, some distant, despairing remnant of prudence warned. It took a real effort to blink and turn her head.

Across a group of people she met Ian's eyes again, and

felt her heart twist at the flash of pain in them. But sorry though she was for him, he had no right to fall in love with her, she thought raggedly.

'I hate this,' she said.

His expression didn't change. 'Then you shouldn't have got yourself into this situation,' he said smoothly, and smiled at her, a slow, sexy movement of his hard, beautiful mouth.

Stifled by his closeness, she glanced up to see him watching the muscles move in her throat as she swallowed. Butterflies tumbled about inside her in dazed confusion; her lips parted and she had to wrench her gaze away.

'Dinner's ready, everyone,' someone—Ian?—called above the heavy thudding of her heart.

'We'd better go and help serve.' Curt took her elbow and steered her towards the table by the pool.

Ordinarily the delectably savoury scents would have coaxed Peta into hunger, but her stomach clenched as she gazed at succulent meat from the spit, fish wrapped in leaves and baked in the coals, and salads that were pictures in green and gold and scarlet.

And Gillian shooed them away. 'Ian and Mrs Harkness and I know what we're doing,' she said, her gaze skimming Peta as she directed a smile at her brother. 'Get something to eat then sit down and enjoy yourselves.'

After filling her plate, Peta allowed Curt to guide her to a table under an immense jacaranda tree. Four other people were already there; they looked up, a little startled when Curt first pulled out a chair for Peta then sat down himself.

Acutely aware of their interest—tomorrow the whole district would be buzzing with gossip, Peta thought mordantly—she tried to appear serenely confident while Curt charmed everyone's initial reserve into open laughter and eager conversation.

A lilac-blue flower drifted down to land on her plate.

'Messy things, jacarandas,' one of the men, the machinery guru on the station, said cheerfully. 'If they're not dripping flowers, it's seedpods or leaves. Don't know why anyone would plant them.'

He grinned unrepentantly at the outcry from the women. His wife accused him of not seeing beauty in anything other than a well-tuned engine, laughing when he admitted it without a jot of shame.

'As for wearing a flower in your buttonhole like Curt,' she said teasingly, 'you'd rather die.'

'I'll bet he didn't pick it,' her husband retorted, winking at his boss.

Curt gave a pirate's grin. 'Mind your own business.'

Without a lie he'd confirmed their suspicions that Peta had picked the gardenia and given it to him, thus clinching their relationship. To these men and their wives, only a man in the throes of desire would have worn it.

It was interesting to see how a master of innuendo worked, Peta thought with raw cynicism.

He leaned towards her. 'Pudding? Gillian's made her special chocolate mousse.'

His eyes were slightly hooded, and although his voice was quiet enough to indicate intimacy, there was a clear warning in his gaze.

Suddenly angry, Peta obeyed an instinct she'd never owned up to before. With slow, subtle deliberation, she held his gaze and let her tongue run the length of her lips. 'I love her mousse,' she said huskily.

His eyes darkened and his lashes drooped further. 'Then you must have some.'

Serves you right, she thought furiously, only to flinch when he took her hand and drew her to her feet.

His fingers locking around hers like manacles, Curt said, 'Who else wants chocolate mousse?'

In a flurry of feminine complaints that they didn't dare eat such wicked indulgences so they'd have to stick to fruit salad, the group rose and went to collect their puddings.

On the way home, Peta broke into a charged silence by saying, 'In the end they all had some of your sister's mousse.'

'It's addictive,' he agreed. He'd just informed her that tomorrow they'd go for a picnic at the beach.

Beneath the vehicle the bars of the cattle stop rattled and headlight beams blazed full onto the house, mercilessly highlighting the need for a new paint job. Laddie sat up and barked, subsiding into silence when Peta got out.

Curt escorted her to the door. Tension spiralled through her and the scent of the gardenia flowers tantalised her nostrils. Each blossom gleamed with a silvery sheen in the soft darkness. In spite of everything, she thought wearily, she'd enjoyed—well, no, that wasn't the right word. Regret ached through her; if only they'd met like ordinary human beings, and this was the end of an ordinary date...

Common sense asserted itself briskly and brutally. He'd never have looked at you, it stated.

At the door when she turned to say good night, Curt said levelly, 'I'll come in.'

Anticipation simmered through her veins. 'What?'

Did he sense it? If he did, his edged smile was calculated to deflate it. 'No one is going to believe that I'll come straight back.'

She clamped down on her instinctive rejection. Compared to the homestead her house was a shack. And if he once walked into it, she might never get rid of his presence.

'No,' he said pleasantly, 'I'm not going to sit in the car. You can make me a cup of coffee and we'll talk like ordinary neighbours over it.'

Ordinary neighbours? He had to be joking. 'I only have instant,' she said inanely.

He shrugged. 'So?' When she still hesitated he said on a note of derision, 'It's all right, Peta, you'll be quite safe.'

'Oh, come in if you must,' she snapped, because she didn't want to be safe.

The Peta who hadn't kissed Curt was a different woman from the one who had; this new Peta had developed a reckless streak a mile wide.

Switching on the lights, she said, 'Sit down, and I'll put on the kettle,' and escaped into the kitchen.

When she brought the coffee in, Curt was standing by the bookshelf examining a volume. She plonked the tray onto a coffee table. 'Black or white?'

Other men almost as tall as he—stock agents, the occasional neighbour—had stood in that room, but none had dwarfed it as he did. And it wasn't just his physical presence; something deeper, more potent than good genes gave him that formidable air of inner strength.

'Black, thanks.' He lowered himself into her father's chair and made it his own.

Sipping her tea, Peta stayed obstinately silent, but when he asked her about the book he'd been looking at she had to answer.

Half an hour later she realised with shock that she was enjoying herself, albeit in a tense, disturbing way. His mind stimulated her and she liked the way he discussed things, with a sharp acuity that kept her on her toes.

And when she disagreed with him, he didn't get angry—surely unusual for a dominant man? Her father's rejection of anyone else's opinions but his own had marred her childhood.

After a quick look at her watch she said, 'I think you should go now.'

Lounging back in the big chair with its faded upholstery, he fixed her with a glinting glance. 'Why?'

'I don't want to get a reputation for being easy,' she said smartly. 'I have to live here.'

There was a short silence while she recalled that she might not be living here for much longer if he decided to close down her access.

With a humourless smile he got to his feet. 'That would never do. My mother drummed into me the importance of not stripping a woman of her good reputation,' he drawled. 'I'll see you tomorrow. Can you be ready by ten?'

'No.' But she wanted to be. She explained, 'I've got calves to feed and move into a new paddock. About eleven-thirty would be better, and I'll have to be back by two-thirty.'

He frowned. 'You work too hard.'

'That's life,' she said flippantly.

She waited until his rear lights had disappeared, then changed and went across to the shed to check the animals. The calf she'd rescued from the swamp was dead.

CHAPTER FOUR

FIGHTING back tears, Peta sat down on a hay bale and blew her nose. She'd believed she was inured to the many different ways animals could die, so why was she crying?

Because it had been a horrible day. Curt had revealed his true colours as a hard-dealing magnate, threatening her with the loss of her livelihood and everything else, and demolishing with brutal contempt her attempts to convince him she wasn't a money-hungry home-wrecker.

She wiped her eyes. And for some reason she wasn't ready to face, his refusal to accept the truth hurt.

That was scary enough, but even more frightening was the physical longing, hot and urgent and uncontrollable, that had engulfed her both times he'd kissed her.

Scariest of all, was the fact that he wanted her too.

The difference was that Curt was in full control of his passions. She wasn't, and if she spent too much time with him desire might deepen into craving.

On the other hand, she thought wearily, surely she had more pride than to choose as her first lover a man who despised her because he thought she was greedy and amoral.

'What else can go wrong?' she said aloud, startled by the thin wobble of her voice in the warm, hay-scented air.

The next morning she was halfway through digging a hole behind the shed when she heard a car come up the drive. Barking importantly, Laddie disappeared, only to fall silent almost immediately.

Someone the dog knew, then. Please, not Ian.

She kept on spading dirt away until Curt asked brusquely, 'What are you doing?'

'Digging a hole.' She concentrated on keeping up a steady rhythm.

'I'll do it.'

She straightened then and gave him a shadowed glance. As she had once before, she said, 'You're not dressed for it. And you might get blisters on your hands.'

He said evenly, 'If you want an undignified wrestling match I'll give you one, but it's only fair to point out that I'm a lot bigger than you are and a lot stronger, and I'll win.'

Peta didn't move.

'So if you make me take the spade off you by force I'll have to conclude that you want to wrestle,' he finished.

A note in his voice warned her that he'd take full advantage of any opportunities she gave him. Muttering something beneath her breath, she slammed the tool into the ground.

'Wise woman,' he said unforgivingly, and picked up the implement. 'The calf, I presume?'

'It was dead when I went to check it last night.'

He nodded and began to dig, his easy movements showing that hard physical labour wasn't new to him. Sensation ambushed her as she watched the smooth flexion of muscles through the material of his shirt and trousers, the effortless power that meant he could do the work in half the time that she could.

Subliminal excitement dilated her eyes, sending exquisite little thrills through her. She had to swallow to ease a suddenly dry throat, and turned blindly towards the shed.

'You look exhausted,' he said abruptly, not even breathing faster. 'Did you get any sleep last night?'

'Not a lot,' she admitted before realising how shaming a confession that was.

Fortunately he took her admission another way. 'How on earth do you expect to farm successfully if the loss of one calf does this to you? Go inside and make yourself a cup of tea.'

She swung around to face him, planting her hands on her hips. 'I've been farming on my own for five years,' she said clearly, 'and I've managed quite well without you. This is *my* farm and *my* loss. I'm not going to be sent off to the house to do housewifely things while some big, strong man does the work.'

Eyes half-closed and speculative, he scanned her face then began to move dirt again. 'Fair enough.'

Astonished, she stared at him.

'We'll bury it together,' he said.

So they did, although he made sure the heaviest work was left to him.

When it was done he helped her move a length of electric fence. Surveying the calves as they frolicked onto the new grass, he asked levelly, 'Why didn't you sell this place when your parents died?'

Peta set off for the house, tossing over her shoulder, 'Why should I?'

'For a better life?' Two long strides caught her up.

'I like farming. And I earn enough to live on.'

'If you did, you wouldn't be working at the local petrol station four hours a day.'

She said stiffly, 'My finances are my concern. The only way you're going to get me out of here is to force me out. But even if I wanted to sell, I have the calf contract to fulfil.'

'A contract that wouldn't stand up in court.'

Although her stride faltered, she walked doggedly on. 'I don't believe you.'

'I don't lie.' When she said nothing he added in a coolly dispassionate tone, 'When Ian drew it up he must have had his mind somewhere else.'

Colour flicked her skin, but she met his hard scrutiny with desperate composure. Her lack of sleep was showing; she couldn't process what he was telling her. 'If that's true—and I'm not accepting it until my lawyer tells me so—what do you plan to do about it?'

His lashes drooped. 'That depends on how co-operative you are,' he drawled.

Assailed by a violent mixture of need and disdain, she sent him a fiery stare.

'What a commonplace mind you've got,' he said pleasantly. 'You're quite safe. I've never had to blackmail a woman into my bed, and I don't plan to start with you.'

'Well, that's a relief.' She hoped the scorn in her voice hid her sudden humiliating disappointment.

His eyes gleamed. 'I wonder if you'd allow yourself to be blackmailed.'

Goaded, she snapped, 'As you've just told me you won't do it, the question is irrelevant.'

He gave her a grin that sizzled through her like honey into pancakes. 'And you've just told me you don't know which way you'd jump.' His amusement died and he was all business. 'I came to tell you that a business call to Japan will probably take most of this afternoon, so the trip to the beach is off. Also, we'll be going to Auckland at the end of this week.'

'We?'

'You and me both.'

How could she dislike him intensely, yet be violently attracted to him at the same time? Automatically she said, 'I can't just up and leave the farm.'

'I'll send up someone from the station to take care of things.'

Her chin tilted. 'It takes more than a written list of instructions—'

'He can start tomorrow. I'm sure that in three days you can teach him enough to keep the place going.'

Suspicion stirred inside her. She frowned at Laddie, who sat back and regarded her with intelligent interest. 'Why?'

'Why do I want you to go to Auckland? Because it makes the whole scenario much more likely.'

What about Anna Lee? Peta almost blurted the words out, but another glance at Curt's hard, handsome face stopped them before they could escape.

Instead, she evaded the issue. 'I can cope with any social occasion here, but unless you plan to stash me in some motel and ignore me, I haven't got the right clothes to carry off a masquerade in Auckland. And I won't accept them from you.'

When he smiled her heart leapt into her throat. That smile had probably charmed the clothes off more women—worldly women, sophisticated and confident— than she'd reared calves. Its blatant charisma was doing an excellent job of scrambling her brain and melting her willpower and softening her heart, and the fact that he knew exactly what effect it was having on her didn't lessen its impact one bit.

But there was nothing humorous in his tone when he told her, 'You'll accept whatever I decide you need.'

Stubbornly she persisted, 'And even if I did have the right clothes, I don't have the right attitude.'

'I don't plan to hide you away,' he said easily, 'and you have exactly the right attitude. As for clothes—that's easily enough fixed.'

Peta stopped and glared at him. 'I told you, I'm not going to accept anything from you.'

'What a sweetly old-fashioned view,' he drawled.

'It might be, but it's non-negotiable.'

'All right, we'll hire them,' he said with insulting negligence. 'I'll want you to attend a gala evening with me, and neither jeans and a T-shirt nor the fetching outfit you wore to Gillian's barbecue will do the trick. And that is non-negotiable, you prickly little wildcat.'

Little? Undecided whether to be furious or charmed, she set off for the house. He hadn't threatened her openly, but if the contract to rear calves for his dairy operation wouldn't stand up in court Curt could pull the plug on her any time.

He had her exactly where he wanted her—on toast. Helped, of course, by the wistful part of her that would like to go to Auckland, to be with him, to hear him talk and make him laugh...

Taking her silence for assent, he said, 'I'll send a helicopter to pick you up on Friday morning. A farmhand will be here at three this afternoon when you come back from your stint manning the petrol pumps.'

Peta saw salvation. 'I forgot—there's no way I can come. I work at the service station over the weekend.'

'He's already found someone to take your place.'

Outraged, she hid a thread of panicky fear with aggression. 'What did you do—threaten Sandy with the loss of the station account?'

'I didn't have to. No one is indispensable. Of course

I'll reimburse you for the loss of your wages.' He waited while she digested this and then finished in a level voice that warned her she'd reached some uncrossable barrier, 'If it makes you feel better, think of yourself as someone on my payroll.'

'Technically, I suppose I already am.' Nevertheless, she felt sleazy and oddly compromised as she finished shortly, 'All right.'

'Good. I'll see you tomorrow.'

By then they'd reached the gravel turning area outside her house. Peta gazed resentfully at the Range Rover and asked, 'Tomorrow? Why?'

He opened the vehicle door and surveyed her with cool intimidation. 'Because I'm supposed to want to.' The cynical note in his voice deepened. 'I'm intrigued by you, remember? Fascinated, in fact; so much so that I can't wait to get you into bed.'

Reaching for her, he pulled her into his arms and bent to kiss her startled gasp from her lips.

It didn't last long, that kiss, but it did a complete demolition job on the few remaining shreds of her composure. When he stepped back she was awash with dizzying and highly suspect pleasure, her mouth slightly parted, lashes drooping over sultry eyes.

The sound of a vehicle coming up the drive scarcely impinged until it stopped a few feet behind the Rover. She turned a dazed, flushed face towards it, barely able to focus on the sign on the door of the utility.

'Tanekaha Station', she read, and the man looking out from it was Ian.

So Curt must have recognised the engine and kissed her to make a point.

Acutely aware that Curt's hand had come to rest on her shoulder, she tried to produce a smile. Her effort was wasted; Ian wasn't looking at her. His gaze was fixed on Curt's face, and instead of his usual expression there was a set weariness in the blunt features.

Curt didn't move; she sensed a waiting, cold patience, the concentrated intensity of a predator watching its prey. And something else, a primitive possessiveness that said bluntly, *My woman. Keep away.*

'Hello, Ian,' Peta said, nerves quivering at the tension smoking around them.

He glanced at her. 'Everything OK?'

'Yes, although the calf we got out of the swamp died last night.' The words sounded unnaturally stiff, almost formal.

He shrugged. 'It happens. I suppose you've buried it?'

'Curt did,' she said. 'He didn't seem to think I was capable.'

Ian's face eased into a wry half-smile that vanished when Curt said urbanely, 'I'm sure you can do anything you put your mind to. It's just that when I was too young to realise I was being brainwashed, my mother drummed into me that because men are stronger than women they do the heavy work.'

A subtle challenge underpinned the teasing words, and the pressure of his long fingers on her shoulder warned her to follow suit.

Pinning what she hoped was a carefree smile to her lips, she said, 'Whereas my father believed women should be able to look after themselves.'

Ian nodded. 'OK, then, I'll see you around,' he said and put the ute into reverse.

The wheels spun at the weight of a foot incautiously heavy on the accelerator, then gripped and spat out a small spray of stones. When Peta stepped back, Curt's arm settled around her shoulders. She stiffened, but he turned her towards the house and urged her with him.

'That should give him some idea of what's going on,' he said bluntly. 'If he wasn't trying to break my sister's heart I could almost feel sorry for him.'

Peta tried to shrug free of his arm, but he turned her towards him, examining her face with hooded eyes.

'Get used to my touch,' he told her, his survey as dispassionately relentless as the tone of his voice. 'He's still not sure that this is for real; he knows damned well that I'd do anything to save Gillian pain.'

'You're a very noble brother.' She lifted her chin against a betraying surge of painful need.

He dropped his arm and nodded at the door. 'Invite me inside. I deserve a cup of coffee for my exertions on your behalf.'

'Unwanted exertions,' she flashed back, but she opened the door.

Watching her move gracefully about the bleak kitchen, Curt wondered exactly what was going on behind those green, gold-rayed eyes with their dark lashes.

His body stirring in primitive recognition, he thought grimly that keeping a safe distance from her was going to test his willpower. He was no stud, but he was accustomed to having the women he wanted.

What he wasn't accustomed to—and resented—was that with this woman he barely had control over his reactions.

Deciding to use her to cut Ian's little idyll short had been foolhardy, but irresistible. His mouth curved satirically as he acknowledged that if he hadn't wanted her he'd probably have simply made an offer too good for her to resist and bought the farm, making sure she moved as far away from Ian and Gillian as possible.

But no, he'd fallen for her subtle, sensual challenge, and now he was going to have to see the whole thing through.

Dealing with her was rather like taming a tigress—her sleek, lithe beauty hiding latent savagery and open determination. Although she hadn't tried to hide her resentment at his threats, she wasn't afraid of him, and she didn't fawn over him.

And that, he thought cynically, was unusual enough to be a refreshing change.

When she melted in his arms her wild, sweet passion had practically tipped him over some edge he'd never approached with any other woman. Acting or for real? A man's body couldn't lie, but women could and did fool men with mimic desire.

Not that he was going to test her. Although she probably saw Ian as a way out of a life going nowhere, he suspected that she didn't have much experience.

She could even be a virgin. His body reacted to that thought with an elemental appetite that took him completely by surprise. Virginity had never been a requisite in his lovers; in fact, he'd preferred women who knew what to do and what they wanted, but the thought of initiating Peta into the delights of the flesh worked so powerfully on him that he had to sit down.

If she was a virgin, taking her to bed would be unfair.

Just keep that thought in the forefront of your mind, he advised himself sardonically. 'Tell me about your parents.'

Warily, she looked up from pouring boiling water into a mug. 'What do you want to know?'

'Why did they come here?'

She added the milk jug to the tray and picked it up. 'My father should have been born a couple of hundred years ago. He was the last of the pioneers.' She walked across to the coffee table and set the tray down on it. 'He decided that Europe was dying, so when my mother got pregnant with me he moved her here from England.'

'Why Kowhai Bay?'

She handed him the mug of coffee. 'He wanted a warm climate, which made Northland the logical choice, and this is a good long way from the nearest city.'

'It didn't occur to him that buying land with no legal access was hardly a sensible thing to do?' he suggested.

The corners of her mouth turned down in a brief grimace. 'My father wasn't accustomed to having his decisions questioned.' She pushed a small plate of ginger crunch across. 'Help yourself,' she invited.

Homemade, Curt realised when he'd taken the first bite. And delicious. He watched her pick up her mug, and wondered what her capable, long-fingered hands would feel like on his body. The scent of the gardenia bush at the front door floated in, erotically charging the humid air.

'And your mother agreed to this life?'

Peta studied him above the rim of her mug, green eyes enigmatic. 'She always agreed with him. She thought he was wonderful and perfect in every way. They were ideally suited; he was dominant—in some ways you remind me of him—and she was yielding.' Her full lips twisted. 'But she wasn't strong.'

He suspected that she'd substituted the word dominant for another, more insulting one—domineering? Dominating?

The thought amused him. If he was arrogant, she certainly wasn't as docile as her mother seemed to have been. 'Why didn't you stay on at school?'

'My father believed that book knowledge, as he called

it, was no use to anyone in real life. He was convinced that modern civilisation was leading the world to destruction, and that everyone should be able to live off the land.'

'And can you?'

Her shoulders moved in a slight shrug. Curt kept his eyes away from the soft movement of her breasts, but a light tinge of colour stole along her high cheekbones when she answered.

'If I have to.'

He looked at her. 'Did he give you no choice?'

'My mother needed me at home,' she said simply.

Frowning, he recalled the results of the investigation he'd had run on her. 'And then they were killed in a road accident.'

'She was already dying.' Peta turned away so that he couldn't see her face. 'I was glad, in a way. She didn't have to endure much pain, and he didn't have to live without her unstinting love and her conviction that he was always right.'

This, she decided, was far too intimate a conversation. Noticing that he'd finished his ginger crunch, she made a gesture towards the plate. 'There's more.'

He shook his head. 'That was superb. Did you make it?'

Oddly warmed by the compliment, she nodded. 'My father believed that every woman should know how to cook.'

'Very Victorian,' Curt observed, an edge to his voice. 'I'm surprised he didn't settle for a tent, an open fire and a camp oven.'

She laughed a little. 'He was unreasonable,' she conceded, 'but he was passionately committed to his ideas.

The kitchen might not be up-to-date but it works. Don't pity me—I'm perfectly happy here.'

He leaned back in the chair and regarded her with half-closed eyes. 'You don't feel any yearning for romance or marriage?'

Peta's father had been a big man, but he'd never had Curt's compelling presence. Last night at the barbecue everyone else had seemed dim and insubstantial, their conversation lacking savour and interest because she'd been so painfully aware of the man with her.

Alarmed by her weakness, she said more crisply than she'd intended, 'At the moment, no, I'm not interested in either.'

His unsparing assessment sent a series of little shivers down her spine. 'In that case you'll be only too eager to help me cut Ian's crush short,' he said pleasantly. 'Are you pumping petrol this morning?'

'Yes.' She glanced at her watch. 'And if I don't get going I'll be late.' She drained her mug and stood up. Awkwardly, she said, 'Thanks for helping me.'

'Even though you didn't need it?' He too got to his feet, his faint smile setting off an unlikely starburst inside her.

'Even then,' she said with a glimmering sideways smile that vanished when she met his eyes.

Coolly measuring, they chilled her through and through.

Working the pumps at the petrol station, she wiped a bead of sweat from her temple and decided that the only thing that made Curt seem at all human was his affection for his sister. Apart from that weakness, as he no doubt saw it, Nadine had got it right. That Peta wanted to kill whatever feelings Ian had developed for her didn't make Curt any less of a cold-blooded user.

Well, not exactly cold-blooded, she decided later as she turned into her drive. He kissed with an expertise that shouted his experience, but was there genuine passion beneath that Ice Man exterior?

Ignoring the consuming she got out of the ute and unlocked the front door. A wave of stuffy air surged out to greet her.

Curt McIntosh was a walking, breathing challenge, and she bet that plenty of women had come to grief picking up the gauntlet of his forbidding self-sufficiency.

Stripping off her petrol-scented clothes, Peta vowed not to be one of them. What she felt for him had nothing to do with love, and she'd keep a watchful guard on her body because once this charade was over she'd see no more of Curt.

Joe, the elderly odd-job man who arrived a few minutes later, was an old friend. He'd been cowman on the station under the previous owner and he knew how to deal with calves. Briskly she showed him how to use the elderly washing machine to mix the formula.

'You shouldn't be carrying those heavy buckets,' he scolded, forestalling her attempt to pick them up. 'It's not good for you.'

'Joe, I do it twice a day almost all year round!'

'Doesn't make it right,' he said firmly.

And he was so concerned she stood back and let him carry them into the calf-shed, watching as he tipped the liquid into the calf-feeders.

Pitching his voice to rise above the bawl of hungry calves, he said, 'Good-looking girl like you should be looking around for a man to do the heavy work. If I were thirty years younger I'd take you on myself.'

'If you were any younger I'd have snapped you up years ago,' she told him, laughing.

His grin faded as he focused on someone coming up behind them. Peta swung around and met a pair of electric blue eyes. Everything about her went taut; she couldn't breathe, couldn't think, couldn't hear her heart beat.

And then Curt smiled, and life flowed through her again; she heard the contented sound of calves sucking, smelt their clean animal smell and the sweet, summery scent of hay. She even heard a skylark sing in the brilliant blue sky outside.

'Hello, Peta.' His gaze moved to the older man. 'Joe.'

'G'day, Curt.' Respectful but not intimidated, Joe moved on to the next pen and filled the feeder there.

Curt frowned at Peta. 'Did you lift those buckets?'

'Of course.' When his mouth clamped into a hard line she added, 'They're not as heavy as they look.'

Over his shoulder Joe butted in, 'They're every bit as heavy as they look—far too much for a woman to be carrying around!'

His frown deepening, Curt watched the older man walk down to the next pen. 'Why don't you run a hose from the mixer?'

'Because this works perfectly well,' Peta informed him with a thin smile. 'I'm no fragile flower.'

'Possibly not, but you shouldn't be carrying that weight.'

She walked outside into the sunlight and turned to face him, her blood singing through her veins in a wild summons. 'Testosterone clearly muddles male thinking patterns. Relax, Curt. If I couldn't do it easily, I'd have found another way to deal with it. I don't force myself to do things that are too difficult; I'm not stupid.'

'It'll wait,' he said, the magnificent structure of his face more prominent. 'There's been a change of plan,' he said brusquely. 'Can you be ready to leave for Auckland tomorrow morning?'

'No!' she said, incredulous that he should ask her this. 'I can't just drop everything and go. Anyway, it would look too…precipitate! To put it crudely, I'm not that sort of woman, and everyone in the district knows it.'

'All right,' he said after a moment. 'In three days' time. That will give Joe all the information he needs to keep the operation running.'

The tone of his voice told her there'd be no more negotiation. She bit her lip. 'How long do you expect me to stay away?'

'A week should do it,' he said blandly. 'And I come bearing a note from Gillian.'

He took an envelope from the pocket of his shirt and handed it over. Gillian invited her to a casual family dinner that night with a couple of old friends. She glanced up, realising from Curt's expression that she didn't have any choice.

'All right,' she said reluctantly.

'It will be extremely informal,' Curt informed her.

Thoroughly exasperated with Ian for precipitating this situation and Curt for forcing her to bend to his will, she snapped, 'I do know which fork to use.'

'I'd noticed,' he said, deadpan.

For some obscure reason this struck her as funny and she gave a gurgle of laughter.

A flash of blue kindled in his eyes but his voice was level and emotionless. 'That's better. Look on this as your good deed for the month. I'll pick you up around seven.'

He swung on his heel and strode away; unwillingly she admitted that he looked like some—well, some demigod from a young girl's romantic fantasy. And he walked like one too, with a lithe male grace that promised leashed power and uncompromising strength. He was, she thought as she went back into the shed, a man who revealed bone-deep competence in every movement.

It might be another fantasy, but she suspected that he'd be able to deal with any situation that came his way.

She envied that confidence. Her father's views had somehow cut her off from the other children in the district; once she left school she'd seen little of those she'd been friends with. Naturally she'd chafed against his dogmatism and his iron control, but because her mother wasn't well she'd had to go along with it.

Living on the outside had marked her in ways she hadn't realised until she'd grown up.

She and Joe worked together until everything was done. When he left she went inside; instead of working in the vegetable garden for an hour or so she showered, and while her hair dried, hauled clothes out of her wardrobe, trying to decide what clothes would be suitable for dinner at the homestead.

Very informal was so vague as to be meaningless—in Curt's circle it probably indicated that tiaras wouldn't be worn, she thought snidely. The only thing that might suit the occasion were a pair of silk-look capri pants the colour of chocolate. With them she paired a figure-skimming top she'd made in a dark, richly dramatic green.

Once dressed, she looped a tie around her hair, now thankfully dry, then stopped. Would Curt yank it out again? She frowned at her reflection before an idea struck her. Smiling smugly, she picked a hibiscus flower from the bush by the garden shed and tucked it into the knot. Back inside, she surveyed it, her grin widening. The silken petals gleamed in an exotic, almost barbaric blending of crimson and cinnabar.

'I don't think he'll pull the tie off this time,' she said dulcetly to her reflection.

The V-neck of her top needed some sort of necklace, but her mother's silver chain was too delicate for the colours that suited her, so in spite of the rather large expanse of bare golden skin she left it unadorned.

She let out a huff of breath when the Range Rover started up the drive. Her stomach clenched and she stopped, trying to calm her racing pulse with a hand pressed protectively over her heart.

'Oh, don't over-dramatise things,' she muttered furiously and strode to the door, flinging it open with a small crash.

CHAPTER FIVE

'AND I'm delighted to see you too,' Curt said sardonically.

Peta gave a crack of unwilling laughter. How did he do that—make her laugh when she was angry and worried and scared?

Without waiting for an answer, he took her arm and drew her out into the soft light of dusk. Her witless body registered his touch with acute pleasure, and every sense blazed into fierce life as they walked silently through the soft evening, the scent of the gardenias floating around them like a lazy invitation.

At the car he held the door open and said, 'You look superb.'

Stunned, she sent him a swift glance.

Something deep and inscrutable glimmered in the blue depths of his eyes. 'Surely that's not the first time a man's told you that?'

Actually, it was. 'Your sister dresses superbly,' she said with blunt honesty. 'I made this top myself, and the trousers came from a local store.'

'You rise above them,' he said blandly. 'And you know exactly what looks good on you. Forget about where anyone's clothes were bought. You'll fit in.' He closed the door on her.

Flushing, she had to turn her head and pretend to examine the fruit trees down the drive so that he wouldn't see how much pleasure his casual compliment had given her.

When Gillian met them at the door of the homestead, Peta felt a twinge of humiliation at the instantly concealed surprise in the other woman's eyes. What on earth had Gillian expected—that she'd turn up in jeans and a T-shirt?

Worse was to come when she introduced Peta to her friends—Hunter Radcliffe and his wife, who lived some distance further north. Lucia Radcliffe just happened to have been born princess of a small Mediterranean island.

At least there was no sign of a tiara on her regal head.

It took Peta only one glance to realise that Curt and Hunter Radcliffe were two of a kind—elite, alpha males with more than their fair share of forceful authority.

Like her father…

The following half-hour revealed that the princess was about as different from Peta's mother as anyone could be. Lucia Radcliffe knew her own mind and spoke it, a state of affairs her husband clearly enjoyed.

Strangely enough Peta found herself neither tongue-tied nor awkward. Gillian's manners were perfect and the princess, who insisted on being called plain Lucia, was a charming, warmly interested guest. And while Ian's avoidance of Peta was obvious to her, nobody else gave any indication of noticing.

In spite of the tension sawing at her nerves, she found herself taking part in the conversation as though she'd known them for some time. When she needed it Curt was always there with unobtrusive support. Slowly she relaxed, until a wail from not too far away startled her.

'I'm terribly sorry,' Lucia said, swiftly getting to her feet. She smiled at Peta. 'That is our darling daughter, six months old and hungry! As I'm the source of sustenance I'll deal with it.'

'May I take a peek?' Peta asked.

The princess laughed. 'Of course! We think she's ador-able, but then we're a bit biased.'

The baby stopped crying the moment she saw her mother, opening her eyes wide to stare solemnly at Peta before giving a swift, triangular smile.

'Oh—she's gorgeous,' Peta said on a sigh.

The princess picked up the child and held her out. 'Do you want a cuddle? It will have to be quick, because Natalia doesn't like being kept waiting for her dinner.'

'I don't know how to hold babies,' Peta confessed.

Lucia plonked the baby into her embrace, standing back to watch Peta's arms automatically curve around the sweet-smelling bundle.

'I think it's instinctive,' the princess said wisely as Peta smiled into the quizzical little face.

The baby's brows met in a frown, but after a moment she gave a half-smile and turned her head to check out her mother's whereabouts.

'Oh, sweetheart, you are delectable,' Peta breathed, her face lighting up when the baby looked back at her and lifted a chubby, starfish hand to pat her cheek.

Lucia looked past them to the door, her lovely face breaking into a smile. 'Curt, come in. Look, Natalia, here's Curt to see you!'

The baby certainly knew him. Smile turning into a beam, she leaped in Peta's arms, little hands working in excitement.

Curt's gaze rested on Peta's face with a kind of sur-prise. 'Here,' she said awkwardly, 'you'd better take her.'

He handled the baby with the competence he showed in everything else, his expression softening as he looked down at her. Peta's heart gave an odd wistful jolt; it was the first time she'd seen him lower his defences.

'She is a born coquette,' Lucia said fondly. 'She even flirts with her father.'

Peta watched the tall man laughing at the baby, and for a couple of heartbeats she couldn't think, couldn't breathe. Occasionally she'd fantasised about life with a kind, gentle man who respected her and listened to her, and in that shadowy dream there were children.

Now, with the impact of a bullet out of darkness, she realised that the only child she wanted was Curt's.

Natalia began to wriggle, and Curt kissed the satiny cheek and handed the baby over to her mother.

Lucia said, 'That's probably the limit of her patience.'

'You and your husband are right—she is adorable,' Peta said, her voice uneven as she headed for the door.

Outside in the hall, something about Curt's steady regard, watchful and deliberate, lifted every tiny hair on her skin.

But when he spoke it was to say, 'You didn't comment on which parent she most resembles.'

Peta steadied her voice before answering, 'She looks like herself, and judging by the set of her chin she's inherited both her father's and mother's share of determination.'

Laughing quietly, he tucked her hand into the crook of his arm. The warmth of his body sent hot shivers roiling across her skin. I'm in real trouble, she thought confusedly. What am I going to do?

Stop fantasising about babies, to start with!

'Lucia can wax eloquent about her strong will,' he said, and sent an enigmatic glance down at her as they walked towards the door of the sitting room. 'Enjoying yourself?'

'Mostly,' she admitted honestly.

He nodded. 'Just remember the whole purpose of this exercise.'

Not exactly a threat, yet his words reminded her brutally that to him she was a pawn, someone to be used for a particular purpose and then discarded. OK, so he liked babies; big deal. Tyrants and dictators liked babies too.

The pain that accompanied her thoughts was bitter medicine, but if it cured her of this feverish desire she'd endure it.

Just outside the door he stopped her with a light touch on her arm, and bent his head. Heart hammering, she looked up—and read cold calculation in his eyes.

He didn't kiss her on the mouth. Instead his lips touched the angle of her jaw, and then his teeth closed for a second on the lobe of her ear, firing a bolt of delicious sensation into the centre of her being.

It was over almost instantly, but the aftermath stayed in her eyes and the delicate colour of her skin. When he opened the door for her and ushered her back into the room, a possessive hand in the small of her back, she saw Ian's face clamp into rigidity.

A needle of pain worked its way through her. It hurt to see Ian suffer, even though she could never return his feelings. Why did things—people—have to change?

When the evening was over she thanked Gillian and Ian civilly and said goodbye to the Radcliffes.

'I hope it's not goodbye,' Lucia said promptly. 'We don't live that far away.'

Not in distance perhaps...

Peta smiled and said something casual and inoffensive.

Halfway home Curt asked, 'Why did you brush off Lucia's invitation?' In spite of his matter-of-fact tone he wanted an answer.

Her face set. 'Because I was there on false pretences,'

she returned on a hard note. 'Besides, the princess was only being polite—we won't meet again.'

'Her manners are exquisite,' he agreed, 'but she's learned to protect herself from people she doesn't like. If she hadn't wanted to get to know you better she wouldn't have suggested it.'

'We have nothing in common. Once this charade is over I'll never see her again.'

'You're an inverted snob,' he said coolly.

'I am *not*.' Furious, she flared, 'Except for a relationship with you—a relationship based on blackmail!—what common ground could there possibly be between me and a princess who's married to a millionaire?'

'You seemed to have enough to talk about,' he said neutrally. 'You certainly didn't hold back when it came to discussing the state of the world. And you share a certain forthrightness. Because she spent years having to watch every word she said, Lucia rather enjoys stating her opinions.'

Peta shrugged, but his words echoed in her mind after she'd given him a cup of coffee and tensely waited out the forty-five minutes he insisted on staying.

'More camouflage,' he said laconically.

By the time he finally left her nerves had shredded to rags, but this time he didn't kiss her, although the glitter in his eyes told her that he too felt the swift uprush of hunger, hot and sweet and fiery.

Whenever she smelt the scent of gardenia, she thought wearily as she closed the door behind him, she'd remember his addictive kisses. And wondered if he was deliberately holding back, making her more hungry with each fugitive caress.

No. He might be trying to manipulate her, but not into

his bed; he wanted her flushed and eager so that Ian was convinced.

She went back into the sitting room, looking around it with clouded eyes. The contrast between its elderly furnishings, chosen for economy and hard wear, and Gillian's house couldn't have been greater.

About as much contrast as there was between her life and Curt's.

'So stop the sneaky little wish-fulfilment fantasies,' she told herself harshly. 'Curt's baby indeed! You must be mad.'

'First ride in a chopper?' the helicopter pilot enquired, stowing her pack away.

'Yes.'

He grinned and said confidently, 'You'll love it. It's a great day and all Northland's going to be spread out like a map under us.' He took an envelope from his pocket. 'A note from the boss,' he explained, handing it over.

Peta opened it with trembling fingers. It was the first time she'd seen Curt's writing, and for some reason the occasion assumed ridiculous importance.

Like him, his writing breathed bold, aggressive power. He wasn't able to meet her in Auckland; his personal assistant would pick her up.

He signed it simply, 'C'.

Curt by name and curt by nature, she thought, chilled. He was probably making sure he didn't sign any documentation she might be able to use against him.

Well, he didn't need to worry. She knew exactly why she was there. She'd keep her side of the bargain.

The pilot was right; the trip down was fantastic. Peta exclaimed with pleasure as Northland's long peninsula, barely a hundred miles across at its widest part, unrolled beneath them in a glory of gold and green, hemmed by the blue of the Pacific Ocean on the left and the dangerous green waters of the Tasman Sea on the right; estuaries gleamed in the opalescent blues and greens of a paua shell.

'We need rain,' she said, looking down at toast-coloured countryside as they neared Auckland.

'Rain? Have a heart, it's summer,' the pilot expostulated. 'Nobody wants rain in summer.'

And there in a nutshell was the difference between city people and those from the country. She thought of the bag she'd packed so carefully that morning, choosing and discarding clothes, getting more and more stressed until she'd realised that no matter what she took, she couldn't match the exquisite simplicity of the clothes worn by Gillian and Lucia Radcliffe.

With as little taste for humiliation as anyone, she hoped Curt had remembered his promise to hire clothes.

He'd remember. She relaxed as the helicopter began its descent. Overbearing blackmailer he might be, but she'd put down good money on nothing escaping that formidable mind.

Besides, he had an image to sustain, one that home-sewn clothes would wreck. An ironic smile tilted her lips; try as she did, she just couldn't see Curt worrying about his image!

His personal assistant turned out to be a middle-aged woman, elegant and somewhat distant, who nevertheless greeted Peta with a smile and a ready fund of conversation as she drove her to a large house overlooking the harbour in Herne Bay, one of Auckland's marine suburbs.

'Mr McIntosh will be here as soon as he can,' she said, turning into a gateway. 'He's really sorry—an important colleague arrived in Auckland unexpectedly this morning.'

'It's all right,' Peta said easily, trying to convince herself that she wasn't gripped by aching disappointment.

Perhaps some of her feelings showed in her tone, for his assistant gave her a sideways glance. When the engine had died she said, 'In the meantime, he told me that you need additions to your wardrobe. I've organised a woman who dresses people to come along to see you; I think you'll like her.' Her smile relaxed. 'Of course, that might be because she's my daughter.'

Peta tensed, torn between relief and hurt pride. 'I see,' she said woodenly.

'She'll make it as painless as she can. I know how you feel; I hate shopping with a passion and so does my husband. Liz always says that because someone had to do the shopping in our household she was forced to develop a taste for it! Shall we go in?'

Far from resembling the Tanekaha homestead, Curt's house was a gracious relic from the early twentieth century. On the path to the front door, Peta's nostrils quivered at a familiar perfume—a gardenia bush spread its white velvety flowers across the path, their scent filling the air.

Another woman opened the door. How the heck many people did Curt employ?

'Mrs Stable, the housekeeper,' his personal assistant told her quietly.

The housekeeper, a wiry woman in her mid-forties with improbably red hair, showed her to a room that overlooked the harbour. Peta eyed the huge bed, the exquisite furnishings, and the magnificent painting on one wall—and wished herself back home. Damn Curt. How dared he go ahead and organise a shopping spree when she'd specifically told him she wouldn't accept any money from him?

Well, why was she surprised? That was what men like him did—ploughed their way through life, trampling anyone who got in their way.

But she was nothing like her mother. Although she found Curt dangerously desirable, she certainly wasn't in love with him. And even if she had been, pride wouldn't let her follow like a dog at his heel.

And to be fair, the assistant's daughter might have selected clothes from a hire firm...

Peta washed her face, and had just finished storing her pathetically few clothes in the huge wardrobe when someone knocked on the door.

Curt?

Consuming eagerness drove her across the room; she had to take several steadying breaths before she opened the door to a woman whose discreet chicness and resemblance to Curt's PA gave away her identity.

'You must be Liz,' Peta said, masking searing disappointment with a fixed smile.

'I am, indeed. Can I come in?'

'Of course.' She stood back, somewhat startled when the other woman surveyed her with impersonal intensity. 'No offence, but I'm not too happy about this shopping idea,' Peta said, hiding her awkwardness with a brisk overtone.

'It's Curt McIntosh's idea, so we do it.' Liz seemed to come to some decision. 'OK, I can see which designers will be on your wavelength, but can I check the clothes you've brought? Curt said you'd be going to the opening night at a gallery and a dinner party, and spending a day on a yacht. He also said that although the clothes need to be good, they should be useful too, so no wildly impractical stuff. And he said that you've got great colour sense, which is perfectly obvious now I've seen you.'

Pleasure tingled through Peta, temporarily shutting down her indecision.

Liz glanced around, spied clothes through the open door of the walk-in wardrobe, and set off towards them like an elegant bulldozer. Peta opened her mouth.

And then closed it. Feeling alien and abandoned, she stood irresolute.

Liz took down a shirt. 'Did you make this?'

'I—yes.'

'Good finishing.' She directed a quizzical glance at Peta. 'Curt warned me you'd probably object.'

'Did he?' Peta said through gritted teeth. Liz was probably wondering why on earth Curt had allied himself to a country hick. 'Then you can tell him that I didn't, can't you?'

Liz gave a swift, sympathetic grin. 'I've known Curt since Mum went to work for him, and one thing I've learned—well, me and the rest of the world!—is that if you're stupid enough to go hand to hand with him, you'll lose. He fights fair, but he's ruthless and he's utterly determined. How do you think he turned his father's bankrupt business into a worldwide success?'

'I believe he had to dump his father to do it,' Peta said with cutting accusation.

'True, because his father was the problem.' Liz looked at her and seemed to come to some decision. 'I'm not telling you anything everyone doesn't know, so I can say that Mr McIntosh treated the firm like his own personal cash cow. When Curt took it over he turned it on its head and paid off the creditors in an astonishingly short time; he saved the firm and most of the employees' jobs.'

Presumably her mother was one of those employees. 'But to shaft your own father...'

Liz nodded. 'I know. As I said, he's ruthless.'

Peta walked across to the window and stared down past a green lawn, a swimming pool and a fringe of ancient pohutukawa trees. Between their branches the water of the harbour sparkled like gemstone chips.

From behind her Liz said, 'But you know, I'd trust Curt with my life.'

A sound at the door made them both swing around. 'Thank you for that tribute, Liz,' Curt said smoothly. 'Would you like to wait downstairs?'

She'd clapped one hand over her mouth, but she removed it to grin at him. 'Certainly.'

Peta watched with tense awareness as he closed the door. Her heart had kicked into double time and the sensation running riot through her body was undiluted excitement. Three days had only served to hone her involuntary response to his potent male magnetism.

'We made a bargain, you and I,' Curt said pleasantly, but his eyes were grey and cold.

Her jaw angled in defiance. 'I told you I wouldn't let you pay for my clothes. You agreed to hire them.'

'It's not possible.' He lifted his brows when she made an impatient gesture. 'But if it means so much to you, you can pay for them.'

'I can't afford—'

She stopped because he came towards her, and something about his lithe, remorseless advance dried her mouth and stopped her heart.

'If you mean what I think you mean,' she said hoarsely, 'that's disgusting.'

'Disgusting?' He smiled and her blood ran cold.

'What's disgusting about this?' he murmured, and bent his head.

Peta froze as his mouth drifted across one cheekbone. The elusive male scent that was his alone acted like an aphrodisiac on her, switching off her brain to leave her with no protection from the clamouring demands of desire except a basic instinct of self-preservation.

'I am not a prostitute,' she said thickly.

The ugly word hung between them. He laughed softly and said against her ear, 'If you were I wouldn't be doing this…' His mouth moved to the lobe of her ear and he bit gently.

An erotic charge zinged through her, firing every cell into urgent craving.

'…or this,' he finished, and his mouth reached the frantic pulse in the hollow of her throat. He kissed it, and then lifted his mouth a fraction so that his breath blew warm on her sensitised skin. 'And your heart wouldn't be jumping so wildly.'

Tormented delight clamoured through her like a storm. Peta couldn't speak, couldn't tell him to stop using mock tenderness in his subtle, knowledgeable seduction.

She quivered, lost in a rush of desire that burned away the last coherent thought in her brain. Sighing against his lips, she opened her mouth to his.

The other kisses they'd exchanged faded into insignificance; she sensed a difference in him, a darker, deeper hunger beyond the simple desire of man for woman. It fuelled her anticipation into a raging inferno. She shuddered when his hand smoothed up from her waist, coming to rest over the soft mound of her breast. Hot, primeval pleasure burst into life inside her, aching through her body, softening internal pathways, melting her bones…

His touch felt so right, she thought recklessly, linking

her arms around his neck and offering him her mouth. She'd been born for this dangerous magic, spent the empty years of her adult life waiting for it.

Eagerly expectant, she held her breath while tension spun between them in the taut, humming silence. Ravished by the pressure of his big, hard body against hers, the powerful strength of his arms, she at last surrendered to her own needs.

His heart thudded against hers, his chest rose and fell, and his arms were hard and demanding around her. Yet he didn't move.

With immense reluctance she forced her heavy lids upwards.

Curt's face was clamped into an expression she didn't recognise; his eyes glittered and a streak of colour outlined the high, sweeping cheekbones.

Her stomach dropped in endless freefall, and she knew what he was going to say. Humiliated, she tried to turn her face away.

He said something under his breath and his mouth took hers again, hard and fierce and angry, only breaking the kiss to say harshly, 'Not now. Not while Liz is waiting.'

Oh, God, no! She whispered, 'Then what was that about?'

'I'm sorry,' he said, understanding the real question behind the words. He released her and stood with a face like stone, withdrawn to some inner place she could never reach.

She took a jagged indrawn breath, but before she could say anything he spoke again, the raw note banished from his voice.

With a remote deliberation that slammed up impassable barriers, he said, 'I have no excuse; I lost my head. It won't happen again.'

It took all her willpower to step back, to look straight at him. 'Do I have your word on that?'

'Yes.'

Her skin tightened; a heavy weight of loss overwhelmed her. She had to search for a response, and in the end all she could find was a banal, 'Good.'

Curt looked around the bedroom and said with formidable composure, 'An essential part of this masquerade is wearing the right clothes. I'm prepared to pay for them. If you don't agree to that our bargain is over.'

He didn't threaten; he didn't need to. That cold, ruthless tone, his implacable face told her that if she reneged on their deal she'd find herself with no farm, no way of earning her living—nothing.

'Very well,' she said stonily. 'But when I leave here the clothes will stay.'

He shrugged. 'That's entirely up to you. I'll go and tell Liz you'll be ready in ten minutes.'

In the sanctuary of the bathroom, all marble and mirrors and glimmering glass, Peta eyed her reflection. Completely out of place in this cool, sleek sophistication, the woman in the glass blazed with a sensuous earthiness, her mouth kissed red and sultry eyes shooting gold sparks.

Even her hair was wild—she looked as though she'd been plugged into an electric socket.

After fumbling with the taps she ran cold water over her wrists and washed her face, then dragged a comb through her hair and with a vicious twist tightened the tie that dragged it off her face.

Another survey of her reflection convinced her that she'd managed to tone down the telltale sensuality and hunger. Now she just looked…charged, energised, as though she was hurrying eagerly forward to the future.

As though she was in control of her life, she thought hollowly.

At the top of the stairs she heard voices floating up from below; they fell silent when she started down. She swallowed and held her head high, taking each step carefully as Curt watched her with an expression that gave nothing away. Liz followed his gaze, her mobile face registering a moment of comprehension before it too went blank.

Acutely self-conscious, Peta reached the bottom and came towards them.

'You're ready?' Liz said, then gave a short laugh. 'Stupid question. So let's roll.'

'Be back here at five,' Curt said, walking beside Peta towards the open front door. 'Don't let them hack into her hair.'

Shocked, Peta glanced over her shoulder. He was looking at the woman beside her.

'Of course not,' Liz said with a frown. 'It would be a wicked sin. Don't worry, I know what I'm doing.'

Curt transferred his gaze to Peta. 'Have fun.'

Peta's eyes focused somewhere beyond and above his broad shoulder. 'Thank you,' she said on a note of irony, and she and the other woman went out into the summer sunlight.

'Tell me about yourself,' Liz invited as she drove through Auckland's crazy traffic.

'I'm twenty-three,' Peta said, wondering why she needed to do this. 'I work my own farm and I lead a pure and wholesome life.'

Liz laughed. 'Not if you stick with Curt for long,' she warned. 'He's a course in sophistication all on his own. Who's your favourite author?'

'Only one?'

'Run through them, then.'

Peta began with Jane Austen and finished with her latest discovery from the library, adding, 'And I love reading whodunnits and romances.'

'Who doesn't?' Liz said cheerfully. 'OK, so you're a romantic. What do you do for a hobby? What flowers do you have in your garden? Or is it only vegetables?'

The vegetable garden had been her father's domain, one she kept up for economy's sake. Flower gardens, he'd said, were a waste of precious time. 'I have three hibiscus bushes and a gardenia in a pot by the front door. As for hobbies, I sew. Every so often I knit.' When she'd saved enough money to buy the wool.

Liz's brows shot up. 'Interesting. You could be a casual or a romantic, but my guess is that you're one of the rare people who can wear several looks. We'll see.'

Expertly negotiating a crowded, narrow street, she pulled up outside a shop that had one outrageous dress in the window. 'Let's go,' she said cheerfully.

CHAPTER SIX

WHAT followed was one of the most exhausting afternoons Peta had ever endured. 'And that includes hay-
making,' she said wearily over a restorative cup of tea in
a small, unfashionable café that made, Liz assured her,
the best latte south of the equator. The tea was excellent
too.

Liz laughed. 'Admit that you thought all Aucklanders—
especially shopaholics—were effete weaklings.'

'I'm not that much of a hayseed,' Peta told her loftily,
'but I had no idea you were going to drag me around a
couple of hundred stores and boutiques.'

'Seven,' her companion corrected. 'And now that
you've stocked up on caffeine and tannin again, let's get
your hair done.'

The stylist took them into a private room. Watching
him in the mirror, Peta felt he spent an inordinately long
time just letting her hair ripple through his fingers while
he frowned at her reflection.

'Good bone structure,' he finally pronounced. 'And
I'm not going to mess about with colour—it's perfect as
it is. I'll cut it a little shorter and show you a couple of
ways to put it up.' He glanced at her hands and shuddered. 'One of the girls will give you a manicure.'

He was a genius with the scissors, but the manicure
turned out to be an exercise in sensuous pleasure. On the
way home Peta was very aware of the soft gloss of sheen

105

on her nails, and wondered if Curt would like the way
they seemed to make her fingers even longer.

No, she thought desperately, what the *hell* are you
thinking?

It couldn't be allowed to matter. Unfortunately, it did,
and the next few days stretched out before her like an
ordeal, one with an infinite possibility of consequences.

All of them bad.

Remember what happened to your mother, she ordered. Unless you're a princess, loving a dominant man
leads to misery. The intense, reluctant attraction she felt
for Curt was only the first step on the perilous road that
had led to her mother sacrificing her individuality, her
talent and her freedom to the jealous god of love.

But her mother's tragedy seemed thin and insubstantial, as though Curt's vitality drained life from her memories.

Halfway home, her eye caught the parcels and boxes
in the back of Liz's hatchback. While Peta's hair and
hands were being groomed, the other woman had collected a range of accessories.

Assailed by an empty feeling of disconnection, Peta
stared out at the busy streets.

I don't belong here, she thought sombrely.

Like a girl in a fairytale, carried off across some perilous border between reality and fantasy, she was lost in
a world she didn't understand and prey to dangers she
barely recognised.

The greatest of which, she thought with a flare of worrying anticipation, was waiting for her in that gracious
old house.

Curt had snapped his fingers and people had obeyed,
whisking her out of her familiar world and transporting
her wherever he ordered them to. She'd obeyed too, be-

cause she was afraid of what he could do to her life if she didn't.

And because you don't want Ian to fall in love with you, she reminded herself.

It was too easy to forget that.

'A good afternoon,' Liz said with satisfaction. She drew up on the gravel drive and switched off the engine.

Curt wasn't at home. Peta knew as soon as she walked through the front door; some invisible, intangible force had vanished. Repressing a sinister disappointment, she went with Liz up to her bedroom.

The next hour was spent trying on the carefully chosen clothes, matching them to the accessories Liz had collected. Peta meant to stay aloof and let Liz choose for her, but somehow she found herself offering opinions, falling in love with various garments, wrinkling her nose at others.

'OK, that's fine,' Liz said when the final choices had been packed away in the wardrobe. 'And if I say so myself, we've done a good job. Those clothes not only highlight your good points, they'll take you from breakfast to midnight. It's a pity I can't tell everyone I dressed you— you look stunning. But in my job I have to be the soul of discretion; Curt wouldn't have contacted me if I hadn't been.'

'I know that,' Peta said drily.

Liz nodded. 'You made it a lot easier for me—you've got excellent taste and an inherent understanding of what suits you and doesn't. Now, forget about all this, and just have fun!'

The faintest hint of envy in her tone made Peta wonder just how well she knew Curt, and whether there was perhaps a past attachment between them.

Smiling hard to cover a pang—no, *not* jealousy—Peta

waved goodbye, then turned back to the house, feeling more alone than she ever had in her life. After her parents had died she'd at least been in familiar surroundings. Here she knew no one; even Nadine had left her firm of inner-city solicitors for a holiday in Fiji.

After refusing an offer of afternoon tea from the housekeeper, Peta made her way outside and looked around her with wonder and a growing appreciation. For some reason it seemed rude to explore, so she sat in an elegant and extremely comfortable chair on the wide veranda and tried to empty her mind of everything but the way the sun glinted on the harbour.

When the skin tightened between her shoulder blades, she glanced up, and saw Curt walking towards her.

Awkwardly she got up, angry because she'd weakly followed Liz's suggestion to leave on the lion-coloured cotton trousers and the sleeveless T-shirt—made interesting, so Liz had announced, by the mesh overlay.

'They show off those splendid shoulders,' she'd said, slipping a choker of wooden beads in the same golden tones around Peta's throat.

She'd agreed because she felt good in the outfit, but now she could only think that the top exposed far too much skin to Curt's narrowed eyes.

And that's why you left it on, she thought in self-disgust.

She thought of his mouth on her skin, and to her horror her breasts burned and their centres budded in immediate response. He had to notice.

He had noticed; his gaze heated and his mouth curved in the mirthless smile of a hunter sighting prey.

A combustible mixture of satisfaction, distrust and humiliation drove her to ask harshly, 'I hope it's worth the expense.'

His lashes drooped and he stopped and surveyed her at his leisure—for all the world, she thought indignantly, like some pasha checking out the latest slave girl in the harem.

It was her own fault; she'd given him the opportunity to ram home just how much at his disposal she was.

'Absolutely,' he said smoothly. 'Would you like a drink?'

She nodded. 'Something long and cool would be lovely.'

'Wine?' Curt suggested, walking up the steps to the veranda.

She said jerkily, 'Yes, please, but I'd better have some water first. I'm thirsty and I don't want to drink too fast.'

'Wise woman.' He poured a long glass of water from a jug with lemon slices floating on the surface, and handed it over. Surprisingly, he poured another for himself before indicating a recliner. 'Sit down; you look tired. Did Liz wear you out?'

Somehow lying back on the recliner seemed too intimate, as though she was displaying her body for his scrutiny. She chose a nearby chair instead. 'I had no idea trying on clothes could be so exhausting.'

Curt smiled and sat down in another chair. He'd changed from the formal business suit into a pair of light trousers that hugged his narrow hips and muscular thighs. His short-sleeved cotton shirt was open at the neck.

So much untrammelled masculine magnetism took her breath away. Peta took refuge behind her glass and fixed her gaze on the view.

'Liz is a perfectionist,' he observed, 'and like her mother, she's ruthlessly efficient. We're not going out tonight, so you can go to bed early if you want to.'

She took another mouthful of water, letting it slip

down her throat. 'I thought the idea was to show ourselves off.'

'Not tonight,' he said.

She stared at him. 'Why?'

'Think, Peta,' he drawled in the tone she had come to hate. 'We haven't seen each other for three days. Why would we want to go out when we can spend the evening alone together?' He invested the final sentence with a mocking tone that didn't hide the underlying purr of sensuality.

'Oh,' she said numbly. Something twisted in the pit of her stomach, a sharp urgency that played havoc with her concentration. She took another sip and swallowed it too quickly.

Curt said, 'I thought you might want to ring and make sure that everything's all right at home.'

'Yes, I'll do that.' She began to stand up.

'Finish your drink first. Joe won't be in yet.'

Slowly she drank down the rest of the water while he spoke of the latest entertainment scandal. From there they moved on to books, discovering that although they liked different authors, they had enough in common to fuel a lively discussion.

Then Curt poured a glass of cool, pale gold wine for her, and somehow they drifted into the perilous field of politics. To Peta's astonishment he listened to her, and even when he disagreed with what she said he didn't resort to ridicule.

It was powerfully stimulating.

Laughing over his caustic summation of one particularly media-hungry member of parliament, she realised incredulously that she was fascinated by more than his male charisma. And this attraction of the mind, she thought warily, was far more dangerous than lust.

He was watching her, his eyes sharply analytical, waiting for her to answer. Dry-mouthed, she said, 'I suppose you have to deal with people like that all the time.'

His brows drew together in a faint frown. 'Most of them are reasonably decent people struggling to juggle a hunger for power with a desire to do some good for the country,' he said, and glanced at his watch. 'Do you want to ring Joe now?'

'Yes, thank you.' The sun was already setting behind the high, forested hills on the western horizon.

He took a sleek mobile phone from his pocket and handed it over. Their fingers touched, and the awareness that had merely smouldered for the past half-hour burst into flames again.

'You need to put the number in,' Curt said softly.

'Yes.' Start *thinking*, she told herself, and clumsily punched in her number, staring at the harbour through the screen of the trees.

Five minutes later she handed back the telephone, taking care to keep her fingers away from his. 'Everything's fine,' she said lightly, addressing his top shirt button. 'Laddie's decided that as Joe is feeding him, he'd better obey Joe's calls. Which is good going on Joe's part, because a lot of the time Laddie doesn't take any notice of me.'

He asked her about training a cattle dog. Later she thought that he couldn't have any interest in the trials of coaxing an adolescent dog to deal sensibly with calves, but he seemed interested, laughing when she confessed some of the mistakes she and the dog had made.

They ate dinner out on the veranda while the summer evening faded swiftly into a night filled with the sibilant whisper of waves on the beach below, and the fragrance of flowers in the gathering darkness. Fat white candles gleamed in glass cylinders, their steady flames catching the velvety petals of roses in the centre of the table, winking on the silver and the wineglasses.

And picking out with loving fidelity the strong bones and dramatically sensual impact of the man opposite.

The whole scene was straight out of *House and Garden*, Peta thought cynically, trying to protect herself from succumbing to the seductive promise of romantic fantasy.

She managed it, but only just. And only, she admitted once safe in her room, because he didn't touch her at all.

That night she didn't sleep well, waking bleary-eyed and disoriented to a knock on the door and the shocked realisation that it was almost nine o'clock.

'Coming,' she croaked, and scrambled out of bed.

The housekeeper said with a smile, 'Mr McIntosh suggested I wake you now. He asked me to remind you that Ms Shaw is collecting you at ten, and that he's meeting you for lunch at twelve-thirty.'

'I'll be down in twenty minutes,' Peta told her.

Liz took her to a salon, where a woman gave her a facial, then checked out the cosmetics she used. 'Good choices, but I think I've got better. Try this lipstick.'

Peta opened her mouth to say she didn't need any more cosmetics, then closed it again. Being groomed like a prize cow for showing revolted her, but she'd agreed to it.

And when she left Auckland, once Ian was utterly convinced that she and Curt had had a blazing affair, she'd leave this whole deal behind and never, ever think of Curt McIntosh again.

If she could...

Liz dropped her off outside the restaurant. 'Curt's al-

ways on time,' she said with her ready smile. 'He'll be
waiting for you.'

Just how well did she know him? Peta mulled the question over as she walked up the steps, but inside the foyer
she forgot everything else. At the sight of Curt a smile
broke through, soft and tremulous and entirely involuntary.

His brows drew together, accentuating the powerful
framework of his lean face, and then he smiled, and when
she came up to him he took her hand and kissed it.

The unexpected caress jolted her heart until she remembered he'd done the same to Granny Wai.

Eyes fixed on her face, he tucked her hand into his arm
and said in a voice pitched only for her, 'That was brilliant. Keep it up.'

His observation slashed through her composure with
its cynical reminder of the reason she was there. 'I hope
I'm not late,' she said, pronouncing each word with care.

'Dead on time.' His smile held a predatory gleam.
'And smelling delicious.'

'The perfume was horribly expensive,' she said
crisply. 'I'm glad you think it's worth it.'

He walked her towards the doors of the restaurant. The
head waiter appeared as if by magic, frowning at the hostess
who'd come forward to deal with them. 'Mr McIntosh,
this way, please.'

Walking through the restaurant was purgatory; eyes
that gleamed with curiosity scrutinised her, and unknown
faces hastily extinguished an avid interest. Several people
nodded at Curt. Although he acknowledged them, he
didn't stop until the waiter delivered them to a table par-
tially shielded from the rest of the room by a tree in a
majestic pot.

With a flourish the waiter produced two menus and recited a list of specials, asked if they wanted drinks, and left them to consider their orders.

'If you want wine with your meal their list is particularly good,' Curt told her.

She shook her head. 'Wine in the middle of the day makes me sleepy. But there's no reason why you shouldn't have some.'

'I don't drink in the middle of the day either.'

It was a tiny link between them, one she found herself cherishing for a foolish moment before common sense banished such weakness.

Peta opened the menu and scanned its contents with a sinking heart. 'You're going to have to translate,' she said evenly. 'I can understand some of this, but not much.'

No doubt Anna Lee was able to read any menu, whatever the language.

He shrugged. 'It's no big deal. I know you like seafood, so why not try the fish of the day, which is always superb, and a salad? If you feel like something else after that we can look at the dessert list.'

'I'm not particularly hungry; I've done nothing but be pampered all morning,' she said, closing the menu with relief.

When he didn't say anything she looked across the table. His expression hadn't changed, but in some indiscernible way he'd closed her out.

Tersely she said, 'Isn't it a little pretentious to have a menu in French?'

Her comment called him back from whatever mental region he'd been in, and she felt the impact of his keen attention.

'Possibly,' he said indolently. 'But as the owner is French, we can forgive her for the quirk.'

'Well, yes, of course.' Feeling foolish, she glanced at the tree in its elegant pot, hiding them from most of the restaurant. He'd wanted to show her off as his latest lover, so she was surprised he hadn't chosen a more public table.

As though the question had been written on her face, Curt said, 'This is the table I always have; any other would have looked too obvious. At least two tables have a pretty good view of us, and sitting at one of them is the biggest gossip in New Zealand, who hasn't taken his eyes off us since we came in the door.' He settled back into his chair and surveyed her with a look of pure male authority. 'I think another of those tremulous smiles is in order.'

Peta tried, she really did, but the smile he'd ordered emerged glittering and swift, throwing down a gauntlet that narrowed Curt's eyes.

'On the other hand,' he said levelly, 'perhaps you're right—a dare is much more intriguing.'

He knew what it was about him that attracted women; the genes that had blessed him with a handsome face and eye-catching height. Well-earned cynicism told him that his first million had boosted his appeal, and each subsequent appearance in the Rich List had only added to his standing amongst a certain sort of woman. Although he enjoyed their company, he'd chosen his lovers with discrimination, always being faithful but always making sure they understood the limitations of the affair.

One or two had wanted more; sorry though he'd been to hurt them, he'd cut the connection immediately. He didn't want to leave a trail of broken hearts. The rest had gracefully accepted what he was prepared to give, and when the time came for the affair to die they'd accepted that too.

Until he'd seen Peta covered in mud cradling a terrified calf he'd been arrogantly certain he understood women well enough.

He couldn't understand why she was such a mystery to him. Green, yet not shy, she held her own, challenging him in ways that almost lifted the lid on a streak of recklessness he'd conquered in his high-school years. She was no pushover—except in his arms.

Then she seemed bewildered by her own response. Was she a virgin? Curt moved slightly in his chair, astonished at the sudden clamour in his blood.

Peta said, 'Which one's the gossip?'

'The magnificently primped middle-aged man with the elderly woman.'

Brows climbing, she gave him a swift, mischievous smile that transformed her face for a second. 'Is he a gigolo?' she asked eagerly. 'I've never seen one before.'

He laughed. 'No, he's not; the woman with him is his mother. An hour after he leaves here, it will be all around town that you and I had lunch together, and by tomorrow the North Island will know you're staying with me.'

Snidely she returned, 'Well, those parts of Auckland and the North Island that are interested!'

'True.'

'I'm glad no one knows who I am.'

'They will soon.'

She said in a low voice, 'Then it's no use me trying to appear sophisticated and upmarket. Aren't you worried that once they find out I'm a nothing, nobody's going to believe that you're interested in me?'

'You're considerably more than a nonentity,' he said, his ironic tone at startling variance with the slow appraisal he gave her with half-closed eyes. 'The way you look is what makes this whole thing entirely credible.'

'You're telling me that only tall women need to apply to be your lovers? I hope that's not the only criterion!'

The moment she said it Peta knew she should have bitten her tongue.

Eyes darkening, he leaned forward and said, 'Not at all. I'm surprised you're interested.'

'I'm not,' she returned smartly, lying valiantly.

He picked up her hand and his touch—so light it skimmed her skin—registered in every nerve in her body with shattering impact. 'Look at me, Peta.'

Reluctantly, she obeyed.

'Now smile,' he commanded quietly.

So she did, shivers of bitter pleasure running through her.

Fortunately the waiter returned then, stopping a few steps away from the table and pretending to straighten the silver on a sideboard until Curt let her hand go. Pink-cheeked and breathing fast, Peta held her head high while Curt gave their orders.

Then he set about convincing the entire restaurant—or those who could see them—that he and Peta were at the start of a red-hot affair.

He did it very well, Peta thought bleakly, smiling like an automaton, trying hard to behave as though she was falling in love with a powerful, incredibly sexy tycoon. Not that he flirted; what was happening was altogether more potent than that light-hearted activity. He simply ignored everyone else in the room, bending his whole attention on her, and it was hugely, headily seductive.

'You were right,' she said, putting her napkin down when she'd eaten all she could. 'That fish was utterly delicious, and so was the salad.'

'Anything else?'

'No, thank you.' She gave a small sigh and forced herself to look at him.

And froze. He was watching her mouth with such absorbed attention that everything around her dimmed and diffused while sensation spun wildly through her body. Stop it, she thought distractedly. Oh, stop it right now!

The pleasant tenor voice from behind her burst into that stillness like a bucket of icy water. 'Curt, dear boy, how are you?'

It was the gossip, beaming benevolently at them both; his mother was nowhere in sight.

Of course Curt recovered—because he'd been faking it, she thought dismally. He got to his feet and the two men shook hands, after which he introduced the intruder. She recovered her composure enough to smile and say his name and then he and Curt exchanged a few pleasantries. Peta was very aware of the keen, not-quite-malicious interest in the eyes of the older man.

'I must go,' he said cheerfully. 'Are we seeing you tonight at the gallery opening?'

Curt nodded. 'We'll be there.'

'Good, good.' He said his goodbyes fussily, and left them.

Would Anna Lee be at the gallery opening? Peta's stomach tightened but she had no right to say no, to turn tail and run.

Outside in the busy street she said, 'You'll have to tell me if the clothes I choose will suit the occasion.'

A large car with tinted windows slid to a halt beside them. Curt nodded to the uniformed driver and opened the back door for her. As she lowered herself into the spacious back seat, he said smoothly, 'I'm sure you'll look stunning—Liz is good at her job.'

'I don't know much about art,' Peta said flatly. Her mother had spoken to her of the great artists, even showing her books that she'd brought home from the library, but only when her father wasn't there.

A sardonic smile curved Curt's mouth. 'Most people there would probably recognise a Monet, and they might know a Colin McCahon because it's got writing on it, but that would be about all.' He looked down at her, and said quietly, 'You'll be fine; I'll be there for you. Moore will take you home now, and I'll be there around six. Put on your safety belt.'

He waited until it was clipped before closing the door. Peta watched him stride down the street as the big car edged out into the traffic, and hugged his words to her heart. *I'll be there for you,* he'd said.

If only, she thought and swift, hard tears ached in her throat.

CHAPTER SEVEN

WINEGLASS in hand, Peta gazed around the art gallery. People chatted, laughed, sipped, eyed each other up— only a few, she noted with faint amusement, were actually bothering to inspect the exhibits.

Her heart contracted into a tight, hard ball when she saw a couple of women frankly ogling Curt. She didn't blame them; he looked magnificent, the male elegance of black and white evening clothes subtly underlining his effortless combination of sexuality and power. Cold panic hit her like a blow, and she felt again that odd sense of disconnection, as though she had stepped off the edge of her world into another where the rules no longer applied.

Then the chattering around them suddenly fell off into what could only be called a subdued hum. People began eyeing them covertly, and while one couple edged back, a few eased closer.

Anna Lee. Peta braced herself and took refuge in an intense scrutiny of her wineglass.

She heard a rich voice say, 'Darling, *there* you are! I wondered if you'd got bored and decided to flee.'

Curt smiled with a trace of irony. 'Hello, Anna. Have you met Peta Grey?'

Her stomach in free fall, Peta turned. The small blonde beside Curt gazed earnestly around and said, 'No, where is he? Should I know him?'

Without a flicker of amusement Curt introduced Peta. At least, she thought as Anna Lee gave a peal of laughter, she wasn't too badly outsmarted in the couture stakes.

Not that her long bronze skirt and silk top had anything like the sexy panache of the other woman's outfit, a startling purple bodysuit with an exquisite transparent kimono draped over it to emphasise her sleek body.

'Why *do* people give their children androgynous names?' Anna enquired of nobody in particular. She sent Peta a glance that revealed her mistake had been deliberate. 'Tell me, Ms Grey, did your parents want a boy?'

'I don't really know,' Peta said, because her father's heartfelt longing for a son was no business of Anna Lee's. Skin prickling at the tension in the air, she forced herself to produce a cool smile.

'Well, at least he got a big strong child,' Anna said dismissively, before gazing up at Curt with a confiding smile. 'How was your sojourn in the wilds of Northland? Too boring, I imagine.'

'On the contrary,' he returned, a thread of steel in the clipped words. 'I found it fascinating.'

Anna's pout emphasised her lush mouth. 'Amazing,' she murmured, lengthening the middle syllable. 'I didn't think gumboots and peasants were your thing.' She turned to Peta and ladled insolence into her smile. 'What do you think of the modern trends in New Zealand abstract art?'

Peta said tranquilly, 'I'm afraid I'm an unashamed traditionalist.'

Anna gave a tinkling little laugh. 'Somehow I'm *not* surprised. Such a pity—you won't find many pretty flowers here.'

'Well, no,' Peta said every bit as sweetly. 'Some are a little too derivative of Braque and the Dadaists, but all in all it's not a bad exhibition.'

'Oh, you've been researching,' Anna cooed, but chagrin darkened her large eyes. She waved at someone past

Peta's vision and stepped back. 'I'd better circulate. Lovely to see you again, Curt. Ms Grey.'

Curt waited until she'd left before murmuring, 'All right?'

Peta turned glittering green eyes on him. 'You should have warned me that I was being used to break off an affair.'

'It was already over.' His voice warned her not to trespass any further.

'It didn't look like it to me!'

'Stop frowning,' Curt ordered. Behind the narrowed, intimate smile he bestowed on her was an implicit threat.

Although Peta obeyed, she was furious and oddly grieved. Humiliation, she thought stringently, had to be walking into an event where you expected to shine and seeing your ex-lover with another woman, one who was nowhere near so beautiful as you were!

She despised Curt for his effortless handling of the situation. There was something heartless in his self-possession, a dangerous indifference that cut like a knife. Yet his smile sent her blood singing through her veins in a swift rise of desire, darkly intoxicating and perilous.

Being in Curt's power chafed her unbearably, because it meant they weren't equals.

For the next hour she circulated with him, meeting people she recognised from newspaper photographs, people whose faces were familiar from television, several she'd even seen on the big screen. In a tense way she enjoyed it; Curt kept his promise to stay with her, and although everyone seemed curious, they were interesting.

And some of the art was magnificent; she found it intensely stimulating to discuss the pictures with people who understood them.

Eventually Curt said, 'Time to go.'

Outside, she was startled to find that although the sun had set it was still light—the precious few minutes of northern twilight before darkness came down onto the city. As they turned into his drive the first street lamp flicked orange, and the scent of gardenias saturated the sultry air.

'You did well,' Curt said, switching off the car engine as the door of the garage came down behind them.

'Thank you,' she said tonelessly.

She got out before he had time to open the passenger door for her, and waited for him to disarm the security.

Once inside the house he said, 'Dinner will be waiting.'

'I'm afraid I'm not hungry. I'll skip it and go straight up to my room.'

His expression hardened. 'You've eaten nothing.'

The thought of forcing food past her lips nauseated her. 'I don't want anything,' she said abruptly, and ran up the staircase.

Although he didn't answer she fancied she could feel him watch her. Safely in her lovely room she stripped the sleek silk clothes from her body and hung them up, creamed the expensive cosmetics from her face, and showered the last bit of Curt's money off her skin.

Only then, wrapped in her elderly dressing-gown, did she accept that her fury was rooted in jealousy.

Not just jealousy, although that would be bad enough. Disgusted by Curt's action in producing her as the woman in possession—ha! How bitterly ironic that was!—she was more hurt by the aura of connection that still clung around him and Anna Lee.

Restlessly she paced the floor, arms folded across her waist as though to hold herself together.

You've fallen in love with him.

No. To love someone you had to respect him, and she didn't respect Curt. He'd seen her as someone he could use, and he was deliberately, cold-bloodedly using her.

When had he broken up with Anna?

It could only have been during the three days before she'd come down from Tanekaha, because Nadine had seen them together just before Granny Wai's party.

Even if he had broken off his affair with Anna, taking another woman to the opening tonight was ruthlessness carried to cruel extremes.

On the other hand, he was doing it for his sister.

And perhaps he'd seen a way of killing two birds with one stone—showing Anna that her affair with him was well and truly over, while scotching Ian's guilty affection.

Stop looking for excuses for him, Peta told herself sternly, walking across to the window. Anna might not be the kindest or nicest person in the world, but she didn't deserve humiliation. Nobody did.

A knock on the door startled her. Breath locking in her throat, she froze.

Curt's voice was coldly forceful. 'If you don't open the door, Peta, I'll break it down.'

'Come in, then,' she said, infuriated when her voice quivered in the middle of the defiant challenge.

He'd changed into a T-shirt that showed off his broad shoulders and muscled torso. To her astonishment, he carried a tray. 'Food,' he said. 'Eat it.'

'Or you'll force-feed me?'

'Something like that,' he agreed.

She could imagine him doing just that. 'I'm not hungry,' she said dully.

'Possibly not, but you're upset, and going to bed on an empty stomach won't get you a decent night's sleep.

Tomorrow we're going out on a friend's yacht so you'll need to be alert.'

She bit her lip, but her stomach betrayed her, reacting to the delectable scent of food with a beseeching rumble. 'I'll eat it when you've gone.'

'I don't trust you,' he told her.

She stared at him, met implacable blue-grey eyes, and knew she was beaten. With a ramrod spine, and shoulders held so stiffly they ached, she walked across to the small table in the window where he'd set the tray down.

Clearly it hadn't occurred to him that she'd hold out. Well, how could she?

Peta lifted the cover from the plate and stared at a dish of scrambled eggs, smooth and creamy and delicate. 'Did you get your poor housekeeper to do this specially for me?'

'No.' He sounded amused. 'I cooked them.'

'Pull the other leg,' she said without thinking.

He grinned and leaned against the wall. 'I can cook three things,' he said calmly. 'Scrambled eggs is one of them.'

The eggs were as delicious as they looked. After the first mouthful had gone down she asked, 'What are the others?'

'Steak and chips, and Thai red curry,' he told her.

She swallowed another mouthful. 'Why those three in particular?'

'Because I like them.'

Well, yes, of course. Oddly enough the turmoil in her stomach had eased with the arrival of food. Anna's reference to her as a peasant popped into her head; she grimaced.

'Did I get a piece of eggshell in there?' Curt asked.

'No,' she said shortly, glad to be reminded of his perfidy. It astonished her how the simple act of scrambling eggs for her had mellowed her attitude. Clearly she was a pushover.

She said, 'I assume my main function on the yacht is to hang on your arm and gaze adoringly at you?'

'My ego doesn't need stoking quite that badly,' he said matter-of-factly. 'Besides, I don't want to ruin my reputation for finding both brains and beauty in my lovers.'

Peta had got to her feet and was putting the cover onto the plate. His words startled her into looking up. 'Don't be silly,' she said sharply, because of course she didn't believe him. 'I'm intelligent enough, I suppose, but I'm not beautiful.'

Curt walked across the room towards her. 'The first time I saw you I thought you were the most stunning woman I'd seen for years.'

Hands clenched on either side of the tray, she stared at him. His voice had been unemotional, but as he got closer she realised that his eyes were lit by a blue flame. An answering flame burst into life inside her.

She swallowed to ease her dry throat and croaked, 'I don't believe that for a moment. I was covered in mud.'

'And exceedingly disdainful,' he agreed, removing the tray from her hands and putting it back onto the table. 'I had to stop myself from kissing that sneer from your lovely mouth.'

'You were as arrogant as you could possibly be.'

'As far as I knew, you were my brother-in-law's lover,' he pointed out, and kissed her, his hands tangling in the sleek weight of hair at the nape of her neck.

Shivers of erotic delight leapt from nerve end to nerve end. She'd gone rigid, but his mouth melted her resistance so that she sagged into his arms, lifting her face in mute, open invitation, everything banished from her mind but the sheer physical excitement of his touch.

Rapturously she yielded to the fierce demand of his mouth, the iron power of his arms, the hard support of his body as he cradled her against him—to her own craving, a longing infinitely more complex than simple, straightforward lust.

Something different about the quality of the kiss should have alerted her to danger, but she was so lost in pleasure she didn't notice until it was too late to react.

'Sweet and fiery and potent,' he said against her lips, his voice raw and deep.

Heat scored her skin, but she met his hooded gaze unflinchingly, the golden fire that smouldered in the depths of her eyes matching the blue intensity of his.

Raw need beat up inside her, wild and reckless, and for the first time in her life Peta understood how the lightning strike of passion could shatter everything—all common sense, all the strictures that kept you safe. With Curt she didn't want to be safe—she wanted to follow this white-hot primeval hunger to wherever it took her.

Curt touched his lips to the corner of her mouth in a kiss as soft as it was sensuous, then gently bit the side of her throat.

Peta's heart filled her body with erotic drumming.

When she gasped his name he said, 'You've got such a lazy, throaty voice, a summer voice, and then you look at me and I see storms and a desperation that almost matches mine.'

His words seemed to come from far away, and she thrilled to the authentic note of need in them, stark and carnal and consuming.

Hunger beat up through her, so ferocious she could

taste it in her mouth, feel it stabbing through every cell in her body.

'I know,' she said, and something in her snapped.

Or perhaps it slotted into place and she knew her mind for the first time in her life. Even if this was wrong—if Curt was lying to her—she wanted him. For once she was going to emerge from the safe blandness of the life she'd constructed so carefully, and follow her questing heart wherever it led her.

So when his hand slid beneath her robe, she reciprocated with fingers splayed across his shirt. But she could only clench her hand on the thin material because her whole body tensed unbearably while he stroked gently, knowledgeably towards the tightly beaded centre of her breast.

'Are you sure?' His voice was guttural.

'Absolutely.'

Curt forced himself to examine her face, trying not to swear because her tentative caress had shredded his control. She'd said the single word like a vow, her eyes blazing, her head held high and her mouth—oh, God, her *mouth*—firm, for all its lush promise.

He had to fight down the reckless urge to grab her, fling her on the bed and sink into her, lose himself in her sweet fire. Clenching his jaw against stark desire, he let his hand fall. 'I can stop now; soon I won't be able to.'

A savage wanting twisted inside Peta and she shivered. 'Don't even think about it.'

His hard, beautiful mouth compressed, then relaxed into that shark smile. 'Thinking is a real problem right now,' he murmured, a lean hand finding the tie around her waist.

He gave it a rapid, sure tug. The belt dropped free and

the front of her gown swung open, revealing that she had
nothing on beneath it.

Curt froze, and she looked at his profile, so close, so
absorbed, the bold angles and lines clamped into a mask
of hunger that should have terrified her.

Instead, her sharp craving exploded into keen torment,
fuelled by his closeness and the dark intensity of his gaze
on the soft golden curves of her breasts. A rush of pride
reinforced her courage; his trademark self-control was
shattering in front of her.

He looked into her eyes. Slowly, giving her time to
stop him, he pushed the shoulders of the wrap back. The
soft material whispered over her skin, licking against it
in slow, delicious provocation.

Need savaged her, half pleasure, half pain. Her breath
panted between her lips, and it took every scrap of willpower to stand still. At last the gown fell to the floor,
and she stood in front of him, tall and slim and naked.

Moving quickly, he hauled the shirt over his head.
Lamplight glowed bronze on his big, lithe body, collecting in pools of light and shadow. The unsparing strength
of his desire coiled around her, stoking hers to create a
conflagration.

'Last chance,' he said harshly.

Peta shook her head.

She expected him to strip off the rest of his clothes,
so when he picked her up and carried her across to the
bed she gasped.

Muscles coiling, he stooped, hauled the coverlet back
and lowered her onto the sheet. Its coolness contrasted
with the heat collecting in all the hidden places of her
body. Bemused, she ran her hand across the swell of his
biceps, letting her fingers loiter sensuously against the
fine grain of his skin.

'That's not a good idea,' he said between his teeth.

Humiliation searing through her, she snatched her hand back, but he caught it in mid-air.

'I like to be touched,' he rasped, and kissed her fingers, 'but for this first time, take it slowly.'

He released her and while she lay dazed with excitement because he was planning a future for them, he kicked off his shoes and undid the fastening of his trousers and stepped out of them.

Peta's heart shut down. Sleek-skinned, powerfully made, he was big everywhere, she thought dazedly—big and experienced—and she had no idea whether she was going to be able to take him. She knew enough about sex to understand that most women could accept most men, and she certainly wanted him, but—

Surprisingly, he understood. 'Don't worry—it will be all right,' he promised in a thick, heated voice, and came down beside her, one arm sliding beneath her neck so that her lips were only a centimetre away from his.

She couldn't control the tension that stiffened her muscles and dried her mouth, but instead of the onslaught she unconsciously feared he kissed the pulse in her throat, and the erotic little caress eased her into pleasure again. She turned her face into his hair, inhaling the subtle, intoxicating scent of his skin.

Enslaved by his kisses, his slow, worshipful caresses, her mind drifted until all she was aware of was the sleek slide of his body against hers and the building excitement inside her—a different kind of tension, one she welcomed because Curt made it so easy.

His mouth and his hands discovered other pleasure points: the sensitive place where her throat joined her shoulder, a certain spot at the back of her neck. Some he kissed, some he nipped, slowly, exquisitely letting her become accustomed to his touch.

At last he said against the upper curve of her breast, 'Not nervous any longer?'

'No,' she said languidly, afloat on a tide of honeyed delight. If she called a halt now she'd never forgive herself.

She lifted a heavy arm and buried her fingers in his hair, warm from his body, black against her skin. If he wanted to pull away she didn't have a hope of holding him, but the pressure of her fingers reiterated her need and her desire and her surrender.

Peta waited, while his breath smoked across her skin, and then he smiled and turned his head slightly and his mouth closed around a pleading nipple.

The first strong tug of suction sent a sexual signal ripping through her; her body arched in astonished response, and a note of wonder broke in the back of her throat.

In one fluid movement Curt slid both arms beneath her back, holding her free of the sheet so that her breasts were offered to him while he resumed the drugging seduction.

Peta had never known such rapture. It swamped everything else, rioting through her in scintillating waves, setting her alight and anchoring her intensely in that bed, in Curt's arms, willing prisoner of his mouth and hands and of the mastery of his lean, aroused body.

When he lifted his head she moaned in dismay, but this time it was to take her mouth, his open hunger displayed for the first time. She responded with ardent agreement, writhing against him, and eventually his hand found the flare of her hips, and delved further into the place that ached for him.

Peta pressed against that seeking hand, gasping when

he set up a rhythm, gasping even more when his fingers entered her in a simulation of the intimacy she needed so desperately.

'Please,' she muttered helplessly into his neck. 'Oh, please…'

'You don't need to ask,' he said, his voice abrasive with barely leashed hunger. 'I'm more than willing to please you.'

He positioned himself over her; she looked up into molten eyes and a face drawn into a hard, triumphant mask. For a moment her heart quailed; he filled her vision, blocking out the rest of the world so that all she could see was Curt.

And then he lowered himself and she felt his blunt probe at the passage that waited for him. Peta's eyes widened as he eased slowly in. She swallowed.

The cords in his neck stood out. 'All right?'

'Oh, yes,' she breathed, and hooked her arms around his shoulders and pulled herself up around him, enclosing and enfolding him, offering herself to him in the most basic, most primal way of all.

Blue fire swallowed every shard of grey in his eyes; his powerful shoulders flexed and he thrust hard and deep, taking her in one strong push that cracked Peta's world open and forced her into another dimension.

Colours she had never seen before spun in front of her, unknown sensations ricocheted through her, and she cried out hoarsely and clutched him, fingers digging into his hide as she clenched muscles she hadn't known to exist around the length of him.

'Peta?' he demanded, easing back.

She shuddered at the fierce intensity of his tone. 'Don't you dare stop,' she commanded.

His expression relaxed and he kissed her and began to push again. 'No,' he said against her lips.

Peta learned that making love was like a dance, a smooth meshing of bodies, of rhythm, of movement, of breath and touch and the sounds of their loving—soft murmurings, the relentlessly increasing thud of their hearts. Tender when she wanted tenderness, erotically demanding when she needed that, but always in control, Curt led her along undiscovered pathways of passion until she shuddered and bit his shoulder and moaned deep and long, head flung back in pleasure so keenly sharp it was close to anguish because it wasn't enough...

That was the moment everything changed; a rough, low sound was torn from his throat, and from then on there was nothing deliberate about his movement, nothing controlled or restrained.

Their bodies fought and melded, struggling to reach some unachievable goal in a primitive mating battle that led inexorably to wave after wave of pleasure so extreme she thought she might die of it.

And then a bigger, more dangerous wave caught her and tossed her up into an alternate universe where nothing but ecstasy existed, spreading through her in unbearable delight.

Dimly she heard herself cry out again before she was lost in Curt's possession. Dimly she heard a guttural sound break from him when he too reached that place, and his big body went rigid and they moved together like a single entity.

And then the slow descent into dazed, exhausted peace sucked her into darkness.

She woke to a different darkness and lay in stunned stillness, trying to work out where she was. She was in her usual position, on one side. She was hot—but not with the usual heat of a summer night. This heat came from within her and beat against her.

Subtle sensory clues wove their way between her defences. A different feel to the bed—no movement, but she knew someone was beside her. When she opened her eyes the memories smashed through, and she recalled everything, from her surrender to those final moments when she'd convulsed with unmatched rapture in Curt's arms.

CHAPTER EIGHT

FOR perhaps four heartbeats Peta clamped her eyes shut, longing to take refuge in cowardly sleep, until the practical streak she'd inherited from some unknown ancestor forced her to face the truth. She opened her eyes again.

Enough moonlight seeped through the curtains for her to see the outline of a male torso, and a dark head on the pillow next to hers.

It wasn't an erotic dream; it had really happened. She had made love with Curt McIntosh.

Perhaps some small, involuntary movement from her clued him into awareness, because he turned onto his back as though he'd been waiting for a signal.

'Awake?' he said in a voice that wouldn't have disturbed her if she'd been asleep.

'Yes.' It was a thin thread of sound, and she flinched when he sat up and looked down at her.

The silence had a life of its own, heavy with unspoken thoughts and a sense of impending doom. The contrast between her turbulent emotions and the lazy, sated languor of her body shocked her. Don't be stupid, Peta told herself, adding with scrupulous honesty, or more stupid than you've already been. You knew he was a magnificent lover the first time you saw him.

In a flat, intimidating voice Curt said, 'I'm sorry. I don't usually lose control like that.'

If he'd tried to hurt her he couldn't have made a better job. Perhaps he *had* tried to hurt her. He must be furious with himself for making love to a woman he didn't trust.

An even more stinging thought whipped across her heart. Or perhaps not. He might consider sex the normal way to end an evening spent with a woman—any woman.

'I'm sorry too,' she said brusquely. 'What are you doing in my bed?'

Irony heavy in his voice, he answered, 'Sleeping, until you started making intriguing little noises and tossing about.'

'But you're not asleep now,' she pointed out.

'And you'd like your bed back.'

'It's not mine,' she said foolishly.

He flung the covers back and stood up. Feverish arousal powered through her, short-circuiting her thoughts. Silhouetted against the windows with dim light slipping in muted monotones over his skin, he was a figure from an erotic fantasy, dangerous, disturbing, and powerful.

She sat up, clutched the sheet across her breasts and watched him stride across to a dark heap on the floor that had to be his clothes. As he picked them up she muttered, 'I'm not used to—'

To making love…

Would he think she was trying to make some claim on him? *You took my virginity, now you owe me?* Did he even realise that this had been her first time? She'd felt no pain, and she was almost sure there had been no physical signs to warn him.

Into a silence that tore her composure to shreds, she finished '—to sharing a bed.'

'I gathered that.' His voice was so cold it brought the temperature down to ice-age level. 'We need to talk, but not now. I'll see you at breakfast.'

Silently he walked across the room. Listening to the

shush of the door closing behind him, Peta fought back the tears that thickened in her throat.

What was she going to do?

'Nothing,' Curt said coolly and decisively. 'Last night alters nothing. You stay here until I say you can go.'

Daylight hadn't brought any wise counsel to Peta, who'd spent the rest of the night staring into the darkness and cursing her idiocy. That was, when she wasn't remembering...

She squared her shoulders. 'And when will that be?'

'When Ian is completely convinced that you have no further interest in him.'

She said through her teeth, 'Has it occurred that I could do this, enjoy my little taste of luxury with you, then go back and tell Ian it was all a mistake, that I really loved him all along?'

'Of course it occurred to me,' he told her with a flick of contempt. 'You don't know Ian at all if you think he'll take you back. He believes he's in love with you, and judging by the look on your face in that photograph you gave him enough encouragement to make him feel you reciprocated. He'll see coming to Auckland with me as a betrayal, and he enjoys humiliation as little as the next man.'

'I did *not* encourage him,' she said, knowing it was useless.

'I know guilt when I see it,' he said coolly. 'If his touch was so unexpected, what put that expression on your face?'

Useless it might be, but she decided to try and explain. 'For a couple of months I'd wondered if something was changing, but he's been a good friend to me and I thought—I hoped—I was reading something into his attitude that wasn't there. I did pull away. When he—touched me, I thought that I should have been more definite.'

Curt said satirically, 'Any discouragement must have been so damned subtle as to be unreadable. Not that it matters now; Ian believes that you went after a better prospect in me and dumped him. Whatever story you spin him after this, he won't take you back.'

An ugly suspicion stained her thoughts. Had he deliberately, cold-bloodedly set out to make love to her, to ruin any chance of Ian taking her back? She stared at him, unable to see anything in his face beyond forceful determination.

Yes, this man would do that.

Fighting back the outraged grief of betrayal, she said steadily, 'I hope your sister realises how much she owes you for your efforts on her behalf.'

'Leave her out of this.' His tone set up a wall between them.

A sensible woman wouldn't have let this situation develop to last night's madness. A sensible woman would have guarded her heart carefully, keeping it safe and whole.

A sensible woman wouldn't have fallen fathoms deep in love with a blackmailer.

Crippled by anguish, she had to suck in a breath before she could say, 'How can we leave Gillian out of it? She's the reason I'm here.'

Curt's brows lifted derisively. 'That's a dead end and you know it. If we're allotting blame, Ian and his wandering eyes led to this, but if you'd made it obvious you weren't interested you'd be safely at home. The fact is, against all prudence and common sense last night happened, so we now have to deal with it.'

She turned away, looking around the morning room. Light, airy, angled to catch the morning sun and a view of the Harbour Bridge and the bush-covered slopes of the North Shore, it breathed a sophisticated informality in spite of the magnificent pictures on the walls. Curt's interest in art clearly didn't stop at small, blonde artists.

'*Deal with it* sounds so straightforward,' she said harshly. 'No doubt it is for you. So tell me, just *how* do we deal with it?'

If he said they'd forget about it she'd—she'd do something violent! Their lovemaking had changed her life, even if she wasn't yet ready to accept what that change meant. Literally, she'd never be the same again.

'There's something else to consider,' he said, still in that forbiddingly glacial tone.

Her heart stirred a little. 'What?'

'You were a virgin, weren't you.'

It wasn't a question and his uncompromising expression and tone told her that it would be useless to deny it.

Colour drained from her skin. Dry-mouthed, she looked at her cup and wished she'd chosen coffee; she needed more caffeine than tea could provide. Hell, what she needed was a good slug of some strong spirit. How had he known? Had she been so gauche that anyone would have recognised her complete lack of experience?

He said something under his breath and she flinched. 'You don't need to answer,' he said brusquely.

Silence reverberated around them until Curt said with unexpected gentleness, 'I'm sorry.'

Why? She almost said it, catching the word back in the bare nick of time.

He went on, 'It shouldn't have happened. At least I used protection, so you're not likely to be pregnant.'

Those prosaic words lacerated Peta's emotion. I can't bear this, she thought, desperately struggling to hold on to the disappearing shreds of her confidence.

Always in control, that was Curt—totally, arrogantly self-contained, his love for his sister the only chink in that seamless armour. Even last night he'd had the presence of mind to use protection.

Oh, he'd wanted her, but although he'd apologised for losing his formidable self-control, he hadn't felt anything like the feverish abandon that had loosened her every inhibition.

Bitter pride gave her the strength to say, 'Even if you hadn't, it's highly unlikely—the time's not right.'

'Then don't worry about it.' He glanced at her plate. 'Eat up. I don't recommend sailing on an empty stomach. Which reminds me, if you're likely to be seasick, now is the time to take a pill. I have a supply.'

'I've never been out on a boat,' she told him, 'so I don't know.'

Another silence. When it weighed too heavily to be endured, she glanced up to find him watching her with an arrested expression, as though she'd said something outrageous.

She said stonily, 'We didn't have money for a boat—besides, my father knew nothing about the sea. I'm sure I'm not the only New Zealander who's never sailed.'

Something that might have been anger tightened his lips, but it had gone before she could identify it properly. And when he said, 'Have you ever been sick in a car?' his tone was casual rather than concerned.

'No.'

'Then you'll probably be all right.'

Breakfast turned into a marathon of forcing food into her unwilling mouth, chewing without tasting, and swallowing without pleasure. After another cup of tea Peta fled to the sanctuary of her bedroom.

For this event Liz had suggested a pair of cotton trousers cut with precision to show off good legs, and a sleeveless singlet in a dark tomato red that lent a glow to Peta's tan.

'There's always a wind at sea,' she'd said, adding an unstructured jacket striped in both colours. 'And you need shelter.' She'd plonked a straw hat on Peta's head and held out sunglasses. 'These are seriously good sunglasses, but not the absolute latest. You don't want to look as though everything's brand new.'

Even with her nerves strained tight, Peta had to admit that Liz knew her stuff. Except for one item; the swimsuit. Spare and sleek, it hadn't been cut particularly high or low, but it had revealed every line of her body.

'Of course it does—and you've got the perfect body to wear it,' Liz had said firmly.

Now Peta jutted her jaw and thrust the scrap of material back onto the shelf. Control of her life might have been temporarily taken away from her, but wherever she could assert it, she would.

The only way she'd endure this purgatory was to face facts—she loved Curt and he didn't love her.

She dropped the sunglasses into a straw bag, followed them with a library book she'd brought from home, and clicked the fastening shut, her mind busy as she tried to assemble her thoughts into some sort of order. Perhaps it wasn't love; after all, what did she have to measure her emotions against? This painful fascination, this feeling that Curt was the only real person in a world that had suddenly gone shadowy, could simply mean that she was in lust.

Love meant subjugation, and although Curt had blackmailed her into this situation, he was different from her father. He didn't expect the mental obedience her father had exacted; he didn't, she thought, struggling to put her finger on the difference between the two men, take any difference of opinion personally.

Curt was certainly dominant, but his dominance was based on his knowledge of his own competence and ability, whereas her father—her father, she thought wonderingly, must have been desperately insecure...

Pop psychology—and was she trying to make excuses for Curt's behaviour? She picked up the straw bag and headed for the door.

Only time would tell; if it was lust it would die once she'd regained her freedom. Until then, the only way to keep what few miserable scraps of pride she had left after last night's spectacular extravaganza of emotion and sensation in Curt's arms was to go cold turkey. Making love to him had been magical and addictive, but it wasn't worth the aftermath.

A knock on the door startled her. Curt said through it, 'Are you ready?'

'Yes, I'm ready.' Jaw angled in determination, she opened the door and went out to join him.

Somehow she'd expected the yacht to be some huge, opulent affair with crew and socialites scattered over it and not a sail in sight. Instead she found a long, elegant sloop whose owners and only crew were a pleasant, middle-aged couple, Doug and Mary Anderson, clearly good friends of Curt's. Perhaps he'd decided that she wasn't up to coping with socialites?

Probably. And that hurt too, but at least with these people she could relax—well, as much as possible when Curt sat next to her and dropped a long arm casually around her shoulders. His faint, potent scent mingled with the keen tang of salt to arouse that hidden hunger in every cell of her body.

Peta had never heard of anyone having flashbacks of pleasant occasions, but every time she looked at him some tormenting image from the previous night blazed across her head. When he turned his head to say something to Mary Anderson, she recalled the stark angles of his profile against the pale skin of her breasts. And when Doug offered him the wheel, she saw an echo of the absorbed intentness with which he undressed her, the complete concentration on her pleasure that had wrung such exquisite sensations from her.

Sensations that lingered too close to the surface, she thought savagely. She'd better banish them to some nice dark basement of her mind and lock the door on them before she made a fool of herself.

They motored out of the marina and then Mary took the tiller and Curt and Doug raised sails and heaved on ropes.

When the sails were billowing to everyone's satisfaction, Peta gazed around at a harbour filled with other yachts and made an attempt at small talk. 'This is utterly glorious.'

Mary Anderson laughed. 'You might have a convert here,' she said to Curt. 'But you'd better not take her out on a cold, wet day when the wind's from the south until she's properly hooked.'

No chance of that; by the time winter arrived this farce would be over. The sunlight dimmed, and to Peta's horror tears stung the backs of her eyes.

'I'll go down below and organise some morning tea,' Mary said.

Peta leapt to her feet. 'Can I help?'

'No, it won't take a minute.' Her hostess gave a swift

grin, letting her gaze skim Curt's big, lithe body as he lounged in the cockpit. 'Stay up here and enjoy the view.'

Hot-cheeked, Peta let him draw her down beside him. 'I still don't know how yachts sail,' she said quickly, not caring how silly the statement seemed provided it gave her something else to concentrate on.

An indulgent note in Curt's voice grated like a burr; to show him that she did have some brains, she started to ask questions.

'Here, take the wheel,' Doug invited after a few minutes. 'Theory's all very well, but you need to steer a boat to find out what it's all about.'

'I might do something stupid,' she said warily.

Doug grinned. 'Curt won't let you.'

So she got to her feet and put both hands on the wheel, looking askance at the dials in front of her as the yacht's motion transformed into sensation.

'Yes, that's good—hold her steady on the compass reading,' Doug said. 'I'll go and give Mary some help.'

He disappeared down the short flight of stairs that led to the big cabin. Peta sent an imploring glance over her shoulder to Curt, only to discover that he was standing just behind her.

Hugely relieved, she said, 'What do I do now?'

She followed his instructions obediently, fascinated when the yacht leapt beneath her hands like a live creature. 'It responds so easily and quickly,' she said wonderingly, and made the mistake of looking up at the man behind her.

He looked stern and more than a little forbidding, but the gleam in his eyes brought hot colour to her cheeks.

After that, in spite of everything, her spirits began to lift. Partly it was the day—sunlight glinting off the waves, the warm wind flirting with the hair on her neck, the islands like gems scattered across cloth shot with green and gold—but mainly it was Curt's surprising lack of antagonism that cast an intoxicating glamour over her.

Towards lunchtime they were closing in on one of the outer islands when Mary said, 'Time to get lunch ready.'

This time Peta followed her down the three narrow steps that led to the cabin. 'Give me something to do.'

The older woman looked up from the minuscule kitchen—galley, Peta reminded herself—her cheerful smile not entirely hiding her curiosity.

'Not if you don't want to,' she said.

'I'd like to.'

Mary nodded at the makings of a salad. 'You could put that together. Wait for a few minutes, though; once we've gone about to head into Home Bay it will be easier.'

Sure enough, footsteps on the deck above heralded the manoeuvre.

'Ready about,' Doug called, and the yacht made a sharp turn and pitched over onto the other side of the hull.

Peta said, 'This is all totally new to me, but I'm having a great day.'

Her hostess looked at her a little quizzically. 'Most New Zealanders have been on a yacht before they reach your age.'

Peta explained again. 'My parents were into self-sufficiency in a big way, and that makes for hard work with not much time off for pleasure.' Or rest.

Although her answer had clearly roused her hostess's curiosity, she nodded and went back to slicing an impressive bacon and egg pie. 'I see. Well, I'm glad you're enjoying yourself, because Curt is a great sailor.'

How to answer that? Peta said cautiously, 'We haven't known each other long, but I can see he loves it.'

'He's also very good at it—good enough to turn professional.'

Peta gazed at her. 'Really?'

'Yes. He's a natural athlete, but his first love has always been sailing. He was in contention for the Olympics until he realised he was needed in the family firm.'

From which he ousted his father after a bitter battle. Peta picked up the tomatoes she'd sliced and added them to the salad. Something she'd read made her say, 'Is it true he no longer speaks to his father?'

'It's not true,' Mary said abruptly. 'His parents no longer speak to him.' Her tone warned Peta to ask no more questions.

But as she tore sprigs of basil into pieces, her mind was buzzing. Gillian must have stood by Curt; was she too outcast from the family? It would explain his fierce protectiveness towards his sister.

The yacht slid to a silent halt and the anchor chain rattled down, much louder in the cabin.

'Just in time,' Mary said brightly. 'We decided we'd picnic under the pohutukawas today—it's a lovely little cove, and for a change it doesn't look as though anyone else is here. You go ahead of me up the companionway, and I'll hand the containers to you.'

Once the lunch had been transferred to the cockpit, Doug winked at Peta and teased his wife, 'I know sea air sharpens the appetite, but it looks as though you've organised enough for an orc army on the march. It's going to take a couple of trips to get all that ashore.' He glanced at Curt. 'I'll drop you and Peta off first then come back and collect Mary and the food.'

Once ashore, Curt asked, 'Enjoying yourself?'

'Very much, thank you,' she said politely, squeaking as her bare feet hit dry sand, fiercely hot beneath her soles. She ran barefoot into the shade of the huge trees and pulled herself up onto a low, swooping branch to put on her sandals.

Curt waited, then lifted her from her perch into his arms.

'No!' she said urgently, fighting down instant desire. 'Not here.'

He lifted his brows, that gleam in his eyes turning hard. 'Why do you think Doug brought us ashore first? Relax, I don't consider the more intimate aspects of lovemaking to be a spectator sport.'

The kiss was hard and swift, close to brutal, but only for a moment. Almost as soon as his lips touched hers they softened, became seducing rather than barbaric. Even as her brain was commanding, *Think jelly! Don't react!* Peta surrendered, and caution and common sense melted like mist on a tropical morning.

They kissed with a kind of desperation, as though starved of each other for years. Lost in the hot clamour of passion, Peta knew she'd never forget the salty air, warm and sensual as the sun's embrace, and the purring whisper of the little waves on the beach, and the long, plaintive screech of some seabird, alien and faintly sinister.

He explored her mouth with finesse that soon transmuted into naked hunger, his arms tightening around her when he brought her hard against his quickening body.

Everything disappeared in the erotic sensation of his wide shoulders flexing beneath her fingers and the taut muscles of his torso hardening against her as he took her mouth in an ever-deepening exploration, a sensual mimicry of the ultimate embrace. Dimly she registered the powerful surge of his heart, the sudden rise of his chest when at last he dragged air into his lungs.

'No,' she muttered, her lips so tender she could barely articulate.

He made a rough sound that could have been regret—or self-derision. 'Any more and the others will find more than they bargained for when they get here,' he agreed, but the abrasive timbre of his words reinforced just how acutely he was aroused.

Not that she needed confirmation; her own body was already ablaze, eagerly preparing for satisfaction.

Frustration tore through her, bitter as winter. She tried to step back and tripped over one of the gnarled roots of the tree. Instantly his arms tightened again.

She saw the moment he reimposed control, shivering when cool blankness transformed the blue of his gaze into icy grey.

'I'm all right,' she said, clenching her teeth to stop them chattering.

He released her, and stooped to pick up the hat that had somehow got pushed off. He set it on her head, then looked down into her face with an intensity that set her heart pounding even harder. His tawny skin was drawn tight over the superb framework of his face, his mouth full and sensuous in the angular strength of his jaw.

Without volition, Peta lifted one hand and traced the outline of his mouth and the flare of one cheekbone, her fingertips lingering against the skin. Fire burned blue in his eyes and he turned his head and kissed the palm of her hand, stepping backwards when the roar of the outboard engine on the dinghy burst in on them.

'Yes, you look well and truly kissed,' he said harshly, turning away as though the sight of her contaminated him.

Rejection burning like acid, Peta said, 'Why is this necessary? I know why you want me seen around with you, but these aren't people who gossip.'

'Why introduce you to my friends?' He shrugged. 'Verisimilitude. If I didn't, Ian would know that this whole elaborate scheme was a set-up.'

It made sense. The Andersons treated Curt like a son, and on the way across the conversation had revealed that Doug, the owner of a newspaper chain, had been a mentor to him.

Peta persisted, 'But why did you kiss me just then?'

His mouth twisted. 'Because I couldn't stop myself,' he said. Not far away the rubber dinghy ran up onto the beach and he turned away, saying abruptly, 'We'd better go along and meet them.'

Desolation, Peta discovered as she put on her sunglasses, was a cold, barren emptiness that echoed through her, shutting out light and laughter and warmth. But helped by the screen of the sunglasses, her wide smile seemed to convince their hosts that she was enjoying herself. They spread a large rug on the wiry grass beneath another tree and unpacked a delicious picnic.

Nibbling a savoury, cheese-flavoured biscuit, Peta thought that it was the sort of picnic featured in the lifestyle sections of expensive magazines; pity everything she ate tasted like dust. The two Andersons sat in low beach chairs, and she and Curt on the large rug; Curt didn't touch her, but no one there could have overlooked his subtly possessive air.

And afterwards he stretched out on his back on the grass like a great cat, utterly relaxed in the sun while they talked of various things. Peta didn't say much, but the conversation had a quiet air of intimacy that encompassed her. She was glad that Curt had found a replacement for parental affection in the Andersons.

'Is Gillian ever going to do anything with her art?' Mary asked forthrightly.

'I doubt it,' Curt told her.

Mary sighed. 'It's a pity; she could be very good if she tried. Interior decorating is all very well, but it's not truly satisfying to someone like Gillian. You know, I think she needs to break her heart.'

'I hope not.' A frosty note in Curt's voice should have warned the older woman off, but it had no effect.

'You don't want to see her hurt, which is fine and noble and brotherly of you,' she said roundly. 'But as long as she considers it to be a hobby she won't value her talent, and she won't ever be happy. She needs to be thrown onto her own resources, forced to find something to make life worth living.'

'My wife,' Doug confided to Peta, 'has a gallery in Auckland. She lives for art, which is why she's so happy to encourage others to sacrifice themselves for it.'

Mary laughed, but defended herself. 'It's wicked to not use a talent. Curt, what did you think of the exhibition the other night?'

The conversation drifted off, and Peta found her eyelids falling. With Curt only a few centimetres away, she should be stiff with tension, but a healing relaxation softened her bones.

When she yawned, Curt looped an arm around her and pulled her down beside him, but this time he left his arm beneath her shoulders. Strangely, she felt protected, as though nothing could hurt her while he was close by.

A chill darkened her mood. Lust? No, this was love, and it had happened before last night, before she'd had any idea of what it would be like to lie in his arms and be taken to ecstasy.

She even knew the moment it had happened; when he'd held Princess Lucia's baby girl, and smiled into her face, and that smile, that tenderness, had stolen Peta's heart.

High on exaltation, she thought fiercely, *Whatever happens, love is a wonderful thing.*

Wonderful and terrifyingly dangerous.

Had this been how her mother felt about her father? Like Gillian, had she believed that it was necessary to sacrifice a talent on love's altar?

'Go to sleep if you want to,' Curt murmured.

Exhaustion and the emotional shock of her revelation must have overwhelmed her, because when she woke the sun had moved westwards and the white heat of midday had mellowed into a golden afternoon.

She froze like an animal caught out in the open, only relaxing once she realised Curt was no longer beside her. Slowly, carefully, she lifted her lashes and peered through them at the swooping patterns of the branches above, the silver backs of the leaves moving like little fishes against the blue sky.

Silently she turned her head and saw the two Andersons, Doug sound asleep, Mary lying on her stomach reading. She looked up and smiled at Peta before returning to her book. Beyond them some hundred metres or so, Curt leaned back against the trunk of another of the big pohutukawa trees and stared out to sea.

For several minutes she allowed herself the secret luxury of gazing at him, embedding his image in her mind. She wanted to be able to recall everything about that moment, from the clean lines and angles that made up his strong profile to the earthy tang of crushed grass and the texture of the rug against her bare legs. Rills of pleasure sang sweetly through her. Last night he'd been all that she'd ever wanted in a lover—masterful and tender by turns, the perfect first lover for any woman.

Tomorrow who knew what might happen, but for today she'd relish every precious moment, hoarding the memories for the days ahead when she'd be alone again.

As though he felt her thoughts, he turned his head. At that distance he wouldn't have been able to see whether or not she was awake, and she hadn't moved, but he held out his hand in a gesture that was both command and offer.

Silently she rose, smiled at Mary and picked up her hat and sunglasses, and went towards him.

Curt waited for her, his eyes unreadable. Without speaking he indicated the beach, and she nodded and set off with him across the sand, damp and cool at first on the soles of her bare feet, then hot and spiky.

'Better keep in the shade,' he said. 'You'll have to excuse the Andersons; they both lead very busy lives, and sailing is usually the only time they get to relax completely.'

'I slept too,' she reminded him. 'Alcohol at lunchtime always makes me sleepy.'

'Half a glass of wine?'

'I'm not a great drinker,' she admitted. 'My father used to make his own beer, but I didn't like it.'

'Had he been drinking before the accident?'

'No. He didn't drink and drive.'

He said unexpectedly, 'It must have been bloody hard on you, losing them when you were so young.'

'It was.' She paused, then added a little less brusquely,

'But death is a fact of life, and after a while you accept it. It brings its own closure.'

Unlike his relationship with his parents. How did he feel about that? Did it hurt him, or had he washed his hands of the father who'd preferred power to the welfare of the people who worked for him?

She'd never know.

He certainly didn't look like a man who held a secret grief in his heart. He didn't look like a man who had a heart.

So why had she tumbled head over heels in love with him?

CHAPTER NINE

PETA'S swift glance took in metallic blue eyes in a hard face. Her heart kicked into helpless longing.

Curt said abruptly, 'I've made a hell of a mess of this. I had no intention of making love with you when I brought you here.'

'It wasn't just you,' she said with difficulty, sidestepping a rock that poked through the sand. From the relative safety of extra distance, she added, 'It takes two.'

'One of us, I suspect, was way out of her depth.'

Shock stopped Peta in her tracks. Did he realise she was in love with him? 'I wanted it,' she said in a brittle voice.

His smile had no trace of humour in it. 'Is that expected to make me feel better?' Then to her astonishment he said, 'Truce?'

'Why?' she asked baldly.

Curt shrugged. 'Because it's too magnificent a day to waste on recriminations?'

Feeling her way with care, she said, 'I don't blame you for what happened last night. You gave me enough opportunities to stop.'

His expression hardened. 'You may not blame me, but I do.'

Of course he did. He couldn't regret it any more than she did—and even as the thought formed in her mind Peta knew it was a lie. Every glorious, abandoned moment had been worth any subsequent pain.

But Curt would know that if by some remote and wilful trick of mischievous fate she was pregnant, he'd be responsible for the child until it was sixteen.

She'd never be free of him; she knew he wouldn't ignore his child, however much he despised the mother. Part of her rejoiced at that idea; the practical part of her shuddered.

But he wasn't really like her father...

Stop it, she commanded fiercely. Don't dredge up excuses; yes, he has good points, but at bottom he's dominating and high-handed. That's enough.

Yet it was sinfully sweet to walk along the beach beside him in the sunlight and watch the gulls wheeling and swooping over the sea, the sun transforming them into pure, shining expressions of energy and grace.

It felt completely right to be there, and how could that be when it was so wrong? Curt had used a combination of sexual charisma and cold threats to manipulate her into this situation, but if he touched her again she'd be lost in that desperate, bewildering, sensual world where common sense waged a losing battle with treacherous desire and love.

She didn't dare let herself be caught in that trap. A swift upwards glance met level, compelling eyes in a face that revealed no emotion. Bracing herself, she took the hand outstretched to help her up a bank.

Instant fire! His hand turned, tugged, and she went willingly towards him, every thought forgotten in a rising tide of hot anticipation.

And then he dropped her wrist and said abruptly, 'We'd better go back.'

Feeling as though something rare and precious had been snatched from her, she worked hard to convince herself that it was much safer to stay with the Andersons.

While they'd been walking the older couple had taken to the water, swimming with the smooth strokes of people who used a pool every day.

'Do you want to swim? You can change behind the tree.' Curt indicated a large pohutukawa.

'I didn't bring my togs.'

Brows lifted, he subjected her to another of those measuring glances. 'Can you swim?'

'Of course I can.'

He gave her a long, measuring look, but said nothing and went off to change. Peta sat down on the rug and yanked her library book from her bag, assiduously applying herself to the pages until a movement caught the corner of her eye.

Slowly she turned her head, her breath stopping in her throat. Last night Curt's sheer physical magnetism had stolen her mind away. The same driven need churned inside her now as her gaze roamed his lean, athletic body, polished by the benign sun into burnished bronze.

Making love to Curt, she thought with a stab of panic, had been addictive; one fix and she was already hooked.

She forced her gaze back to the page, but the print danced crazily, and in a few seconds her eyes wandered again. He was swimming across the bay, strong arms cutting through the water as though he had something to prove. Her body tightened, and then loosened in subtle, inviting places. Into her mind there stole the memory of how it had felt to lie in his arms, with the weight of his magnificent body on hers…

Desire swamped her in a yearning, irresistible wave. For the first time in her life she was gripped by a reckless hunger to seize life with both hands and wring all the juice from it, careless of what might follow.

You did that last night, she reminded herself austerely,

and now you're afraid you might be pregnant, even though you know it's a hundred-to-one chance. The image of a small child with Curt's splendid bone structure formed in her mind; she recalled the soft, lively feel of Lucia's baby, her sweet scent and charming, triangular smile.

No, she thought, sick with fear at the amount of effort she needed to banish the fancy.

She closed her eyes, forcing herself to face something she'd been resolutely ignoring. From now on, living next door to Tanekaha would be hell. Every time she looked out of her window or gazed across her paddocks she'd remember, and every time she heard his name she'd hurt. Breathing in deeply, she looped her arms around her knees and hid her face in them.

When she got home again, she'd sell the farm to Curt if he wanted it, to whoever would buy it otherwise. Then she'd leave Kowhai Bay—leave Northland, in fact, and make another life.

The decision should have panicked her because she had nothing but her knowledge of farming to offer a prospective employer.

Instead, all she could think of was that breaking every fragile link to Curt would hurt like nothing else she'd ever endured. Setting her jaw, she straightened. She'd coped with her parents' death; she'd deal with this too.

But when she looked out to sea the water glittered so much it hurt her eyes.

Curt came out of the water after the Andersons had joined her on the rug.

'I'll bet he isn't even panting,' Mary observed, eyeing him with an appreciation that held nothing maternal.

Her husband laughed. 'Of course he isn't.'

Peta pretended to flick through her novel while Curt

walked up to them, not looking up until he picked up his towel to dry off the surplus water. 'You don't know what you missed,' he said to her.

She swallowed to free her throat of an obstruction and returned, 'I don't miss twenty minutes of hard swimming, believe me. I like to lie and float, not wear myself out.'

'Piker,' he said evenly, and turned towards the tree.

Peta went rigid. Oh, God, she thought, and then, Oh, hell!

Scored across his back were the imprints of her nails from that final agony of pleasure. Colour burned up through her skin; she didn't dare look at the other couple, but they'd have had to be blind not to see those betraying marks.

When Mary broke the silence with some remark about the wind having changed, she breathed again, but the glory of the day had been dimmed, and for the rest of the afternoon she was on edge.

In a way, it was a relief when they arrived back at Curt's house.

The telephone was ringing as they walked in. 'Leave it,' he said sharply. 'We need to talk.'

But it rang insistently until the answering machine clicked in and a woman's voice said urgently, 'Curt, please answer. It's your mother here and your father's very ill. He wants—oh, Curt, he wants to see you. Please come.'

Curt wrenched the receiver off its cradle and barked into it, 'Where?'

'Oh, Curt, thank God. At home, darling, but please—' Her voice was abruptly silenced as he switched off the answering machine and listened, the skin tightening over the strong bones of his face.

Eventually he said, 'All right, I'll bring her over. Just keep being brave, Mother, until I get there.'

An oddly formal way to address his mother, Peta thought. She said as he hung up, 'I'm so sorry, Curt.'

'You're to come with me,' he said.

Appalled, she met his iron-hard gaze. 'Your mother won't want me at such a time.'

'My father wants to see you.' When she didn't move he reached out and took her by the elbow, guiding her inexorably towards the door. 'I'm not going to deny him anything he wants. His heart is failing.'

His parents lived only ten minutes' drive away in a handsome apartment block that overlooked the Viaduct Basin, a cosmopolitan, vibrant area where the crews and owners of super-yachts mingled with locals to sample the excellent and eclectic selection of cafés and restaurants.

Curt didn't speak until they parked in the visitors' car park. 'My parents and I haven't been on good terms for the past ten years. In fact, this is the first time I'll have spoken to them since I took over the firm. I had to depose him to do it and he never forgave me for it.'

'I'm sorry,' she said, wrenched by sympathy. 'But— why does he want to see me?'

He waited until they were in a lift before saying harshly, 'Probably to find out what sort of woman you are.'

'Why should he think I'm any different from any of your other lovers?' she asked, genuinely puzzled.

'None of them has ever moved in with me.'

'But I haven't—'

'As far as anyone knows, you have.'

The lift stopped and he stepped back to let her out before setting off down an opulently decorated corridor. When he pressed the silent bell on one door, a woman opened it and fell into his arms, clinging to him as she wept.

'Oh, thank God,' she said through her tears. 'Come in, quickly. Gillian and Ian are on their way down.'

Hugh McIntosh was propped up in a bed with a nurse taking his pulse; he looked like an older, exhausted Curt with a self-indulgent twist to his mouth. When they walked in, his eyes opened.

'Leave us alone.' His voice was dry and thin, and his chest heaved with each word. When the nurse began to object he said, 'I'm dying, damn you. I want some privacy while I do it.'

Manacling Peta's hand, Curt said to his father, 'It's not like you to give up.' He stopped by the bed and looked down at his father, no emotion showing on his face.

A painful smile flickered around his father's lips. 'So this is your latest.'

'No,' Curt said uncompromisingly. 'This is Peta Grey. She lives next to Gillian and Ian, and she has a mind of her own and a nasty tongue.'

The dying man looked at Peta. She said quietly, 'Only when it's necessary.'

His chest heaved again. Panic-stricken, Peta looked around for the nurse, only to realise that he was laughing.

'Good.' Losing interest in her, he transferred his tired gaze to his son. 'Sorry,' he said. 'Stupid of me—never hold grudges, Curt. Cutting off your nose...'

His voice trailed away and he closed his eyes. Mrs McIntosh gave a choked sob and took his hand, clutching it in both of hers as though she could will life into him.

Curt pressed the buzzer, and as the nurse hurried back in he said to Peta, 'You don't need to stay.'

Outside the room she stopped and looked around, wondering what she should do. Go back to Curt's house? Go home to Kowhai Bay? An outsider in a purely family drama, she had no place here.

She found her way into a sitting room overlooking a large garden bright with jacaranda trees and shady walks. A fountain bubbled in the afternoon sun, and several people were playing *petanque* on a white pitch while others watched from the shade of the trees.

Hovering beside the window, she tried to think. She'd left her money in her other bag that morning, so a taxi to Curt's house was out. Should she walk back? Mentally retracing the route, she thought she'd probably be able to find her way.

But she'd have to interrupt their painful vigil to ask him for the key, and it seemed cowardly to leave him, like running away when he needed her. A painful smile creased her cheeks. Curt didn't need anyone, but she couldn't go.

She sat down on one of the comfortable recliners on the terrace and prepared to wait things out.

When Gillian and Ian arrived a few minutes later she let them in, ignored by Gillian but aware of Ian's strained glance. After that she watched the sun go down and the dusk fall.

The first Peta knew of Hugh McIntosh's death was when she was scooped up by a pair of strong arms. Disoriented, she smiled sleepily at Curt and snuggled into his chest.

His embrace tightened. 'I'll take you home,' he said in a rasping voice that reverberated through her.

'Mmm.' Then she remembered. Stiffening, she looked up into his face.

Lines of tiredness engraved it, and she could have cried for him. She lifted her hand and held it to his cheek, offering mute sympathy. The soft abrasion of his beard tickled when he turned his head and kissed the palm.

'Is she all right?' Ian's voice, carefully neutral.

'She's damp, but she'll be fine.' Curt walked into the room.

'You can put me down,' she said, blinking at the light.

'Why?'

'Because I'm awake now.'

Tear-stained and pale, Gillian said, 'Let him carry you, Peta. He needs to do something.'

But he set her on her feet. When she staggered a little, his arm hooked around her shoulders to support her.

'All right?' he asked.

She looked at him and then at Gillian. 'I'm so sorry,' she said quietly.

Gillian's smile wavered and she choked back a sob. 'Yes,' she said quietly. 'Thank you.'

Curt nodded at his sister and brother-in-law. 'Go to bed, both of you,' he ordered. 'I'll be in touch in the morning.'

Once they were in the lift he leaned back against the wall and closed his eyes. 'I don't know how many times in the last ten years I've asked myself if I could have done anything else, but I couldn't see a way of saving the company that didn't involve getting rid of him. And I knew right from the start that he wouldn't go easily.' Raw anger hardened each word. He straightened up and opened his eyes and looked at her. 'I'd do it again if I had to, even knowing how vindictive he could be. I haven't spoken to my mother all those years—he made her choose between us—and when Gillian lent me her trust money, he banished her too.'

'You slashed his pride to ribbons,' Peta said quietly. 'But I'll bet that as often as you wondered how you could have changed the way you deposed him, he wondered if he could win his family back without humbling himself.'

He gave her a keen glance. The lift sighed to a halt and he ushered her into the foyer. Outside the air was tangy with salt and perfumed by the trees and plants in the front gardens of the ground-floor apartments.

As they reached the car park Curt said, 'What makes you say that?'

'My father was proud too. He thought he knew best and wouldn't accept that my mother was too delicate for his dream. She wasn't tall and strapping like me—I take after him. She was slight and frail and although she did her best she could never quite live up to his expectations. She tried to hide what they both saw as her weaknesses from him, but he demanded such a lot...'

The lights on Curt's car flashed as he pressed the door opener. Once inside, driving slowly through the dark streets, he said, 'Did she hide the symptoms of her illness?'

A long breath shuddered through Peta's lips. 'Yes, until too late. He was utterly devastated, because in spite of everything, he loved her. I'll bet your father loved you too.'

'Two weak men,' Curt said quietly.

She gave him an astonished glance. *Weak?*

Her mouth opened but she closed it again before refuting his remark.

Weak. Of course. How could she not have seen it before? Her father had been unable to deal with reality, so he'd constructed a fantasy world around his family, only to have it shatter into tragedy.

'Yes,' she said on a long sigh as something hard and intransigent inside her melted. 'Yes,' she said again.

How strange that she should owe this insight to Curt.

Back at his house the scent of gardenias floated into her nostrils, sweetly seductive, powerfully erotic.

'Do you want me to carry you in?' he asked.

'No, I'm fine. How—how is your mother?'

'He apologised,' Curt said. 'It made her whole again. She'll grieve, but now she no longer has to tear herself in two she'll be all right.' He unlocked the door. 'At least he tried to make up for what he'd done.'

'Yes.'

He had retreated into some distant region where she couldn't reach him. After he'd bidden her a formal good night and left her at the door of her room, she thought sadly that she'd never reached him except in the most basic way, and he didn't want sex tonight; he wanted comfort. Only Curt wouldn't accept comfort from anyone.

Exhaustion knocked her out before she had time to mull over the events of the night, but when she arrived down to breakfast she'd made a decision.

'I should go home,' she said to Curt once she'd sat down.

He frowned. 'No. It will look odd if you leave now.' His expression hardened. 'People will wonder why my lover isn't by my side comforting me.'

Peta decided that she preferred him withdrawn and grieving. Was he angry with himself for revealing so much to her?

Stiffly, she returned, 'Very well, then, but I'll have to make arrangements for the farm.'

'I'll do that.'

The lingering freshness of a slice of mango turned metallic in her mouth. 'Won't you have other things to do?'

'A few.' He drank some coffee. 'My father had everything organised. He stayed a control freak until the end.'

'Or perhaps he just wanted to make things as easy for your mother as he could,' she said gently.

'Possibly.'

The next three days were forever etched in Peta's mind as the most difficult she'd endured, after those that followed her parents' deaths. Although she couldn't grieve for Hugh McIntosh, she hated the bleak ice of Curt's eyes. He didn't touch her, and the edgy antagonism that had characterised their conversation disappeared behind a shield of aloof reserve.

The huge funeral was nerve-racking; so was the wake afterwards, when she was introduced to a swarm of strangers. At least she felt reasonably confident under the avid eyes and probing little questions, thanks to Curt, who never left her alone, and Liz, who'd come up trumps again with a subdued, superbly cut summer suit.

But eventually it was over. When everyone had gone Curt said abruptly, 'Get into some other clothes and we'll go for a drive. I need fresh air, and I imagine you do too.'

Peta's head came up, but her anger subsided when she saw the weariness in his face. 'Where?'

'Out to Piha.'

She changed into a pair of shorts she'd brought from the farm, and a T-shirt. Neither spoke as they took the road to the west-coast beach, but once she got there she exclaimed out loud.

'Have you never been here before?'

'No,' she said, gazing around. 'It's beautiful.'

'It's dangerous. Look at those waves—they're gentle enough today, but the rip is always waiting. More people die on Piha than any other beach in New Zealand. Let's walk.'

They paced along the beach as the sun went down in

a glory of crimson and scarlet around a sombre cloud-bank painted deep purple and brooding grey.

After twenty minutes of silence Curt said, 'My father left you half a million dollars.'

Astounded, unable to believe she'd heard correctly, Peta stopped. 'What?'

He smiled with such cynicism it burned into her soul. 'You heard.'

Half a million dollars? What on earth had persuaded the man to do that? Shaking her head, she asked woodenly, 'Why?'

'The family don't intend to contest it.' When she said nothing he added dispassionately, 'It's all yours.'

Her jaw dropped. He watched her with eyes that registered nothing but cold indifference. Peta grabbed for enough control to say something—anything—but in the end could only blurt raggedly, 'I don't understand.'

Curt shrugged as though it didn't matter. 'Do you need to? It will solve all your problems.'

Anger broke through her astonishment, rapidly followed by a chill that seeped up from her bones. They had laughed together, found pleasure in talking together, loved together, and yet he still believed she'd take the money. He hadn't changed his mind about her at all, whereas she—oh, she couldn't bear to look into a future that didn't hold him.

But it had to be done, because Curt would never trust her.

'I don't want it,' she said, heart breaking into shards in her breast.

Curt's brows shot up but he said coolly, 'You don't need to make up your mind so fast. I'm sure you'll see things differently after a few days.'

Wounded in some inner part of her that had never seen the light of day before, she said, 'I won't.'

But she knew it was no use. Hopes she didn't even know she'd been cherishing crumbled into dust, and she gave up on a dream she'd refused to recognise.

Curt gazed out to sea, the final rays of the sun gilding his face so that he looked like some warrior of old, fierce, ruthless, and utterly compelling.

I love him, Peta thought, and his father has just made it impossible for anything to come of it.

No, it wasn't fair to blame Hugh McIntosh. Love, she thought bitterly, was a matter of trust, and Curt didn't trust her. He'd never trust her.

'How long have you known about this?' she asked jaggedly.

'He told us before he died.'

So that was the reason for his withdrawal. What game had his father been playing? At least her own father had never toyed with strangers' lives. 'I want to go home,' she said quietly. 'Back to Kowhai Bay. Now.'

He nodded. 'All right.'

CHAPTER TEN

PETA threw an armful of yellowing leaves onto the compost heap. The dwarf beans had stopped producing, but she wouldn't be planting anything in their place because tomorrow she'd be gone and the vegetable garden would be Joe's concern.

Dusting dirt from her hands, she set off for the house. The carrier was arriving the next morning to collect her furniture and take it to a storage facility in the nearest sizeable town.

A year ago—even a couple of months ago—she'd have been shattered, but at exactly this time a month ago she'd said goodbye to Curt and left him forever. Since then very little had managed to break through the fog of desolation that cut her off from any other emotion.

Before she'd been carried off by his helicopter, he'd made one request.

'Let me know that you're not pregnant,' he said, and scribbled a number onto a piece of paper and given it to her. 'That will reach me.' He'd paused and looked at her with hard, implacable eyes. 'And if by some remote chance you are pregnant, I want to know that too.'

A couple of weeks later she'd opened a magazine in the supermarket to see a photograph of him at a gala polo match with Anna Lee hanging off his arm, very much the woman in possession.

That was when Peta knew she'd been right to sell her land. Self-defence had driven the decision; every time she looked across Tanekaha's lush paddocks, a rage of grief broke through her apathy.

It had sold fast. The day after she'd put the farm on the market the land agent had rung her, crowing, 'You'll never guess! I've got a firm offer for you—no bargaining, no hassles. You see, I was right to suggest you put a decent price on it instead of letting it go for peanuts.'

'Who wants to buy it?'

'Oh, some entity in Wellington. It must be for investment because they're even prepared to lease the land to you for a peppercorn rental until you finish out your calf-rearing contract. Now, I *was* right, wasn't I, when I told them it would be four months?'

'Yes, you were right.'

Another four months of living next door to Curt's station.

But when she'd rung Ian as a matter of courtesy to let him know the details, he'd suggested that if she wanted to leave straightaway he could send Joe up to take over.

'We could come to some arrangement over the contract,' he said diffidently. 'You've done a good job with those calves—the rest of the contract payment can be a bonus. Moving is always an expensive business.'

Instinctive revulsion at accepting unearned money from Curt led to her stiff answer. 'No, thanks, but if you're happy for Joe to do it, then I'm sure the new owners would transfer the lease.'

And she could take her wounded heart away and never come back. Time fixed everything, so people said; it couldn't happen soon enough for her. She longed for the day when she could say Curt's name without a quiver of emotion.

Ian had said, 'I'll see to it, then.'

He was probably relieved to get rid of her; Gillian certainly would be.

Not as glad as she would be to go. She'd expected grief, but this vast, freezing vacuum turned the days into blanks and each night into an eternity.

A week after she'd signed the sale documents, she'd rung Curt to confirm that she wasn't pregnant. Like her, he'd been cool, noncommittal and aloof, finishing the brief conversation by wishing her the best for the future. Neither had mentioned the letter she'd written to the executor of Hugh McIntosh's estate refusing his bequest.

Of course Curt might not have known about it; the executor was someone from a law firm in Auckland.

Laddie's bark swivelled her head around. Joe had offered to take the dog too, which was a relief; both man and animal would enjoy the change of ownership.

Frowning, she watched Ian's ute come up the hill. A wild hope flared, dashed the moment she recognised Ian behind the wheel. She steeled herself to walk across the lawn and wait at the gate while he pulled up and got out.

'Are you all right? You look tired,' he said, his face shaded by his hat.

Tired, heartbroken—whatever. 'I'm busy packing.' She waited, and when he didn't say anything her brows rose. 'What do you want, Ian?'

'We're moving on, Gillian and I.'

She pretended an interest she didn't feel. 'Where to?'

'We've bought a hill-country station in Poverty Bay.'

With part of Gillian's inheritance, presumably. Peta said steadily, 'I wish you both the very best of luck.'

Looking uncomfortable, he shrugged. 'Thank you. It's a new start in our own place, and Gillian has friends on the East Coast. I—well, I hope your new start is successful too.'

Peta could think of nothing to say so she repeated his answer to her good wishes. 'Thank you.'

'Where are you going?'

Nowhere, into nothing. 'I'm having a short holiday,' she said, 'and after that I'll see about a job.'

'Doing what?'

Of course, he knew about the half-million dollars his father-in-law had willed her. Did he know she'd turned it down? Resentment flared fitfully in her, then died in ashes. It didn't matter; she no longer cared what anyone in the McIntosh family thought of her.

She summoned a bright, meaningless smile. 'Don't worry about me, Ian. I'll be fine.'

'Have you heard from Curt lately?'

The unexpectedness of his question drove the breath from her lungs. It took all her strength to keep her expression under control and her voice steady. 'I was speaking to him a few days ago. Why?'

'I just wondered.' He almost shuffled his feet, but finally held out his hand. 'Good luck, Peta.'

They shook hands and he got back into the ute. As he drove away, she asked herself what on earth all that had been about. Did he harbour some resentment towards her for falling under Curt's spell? Perhaps he'd come to tell her that Curt and Anna were still an item, but hadn't had the courage to do so.

Or perhaps he'd just wanted to say goodbye, she thought drearily, stopping beside the gardenia bush, another thing that reminded her too much of Curt. One solitary blossom lingered amongst the glossy foliage; she picked it, holding it in her cupped fingers. The scent rose in the warm air—heavy, evocative, as disturbingly potent as the memory of ecstasy.

If it hadn't been for Ian she'd probably never have met Curt; certainly never been blackmailed by him.

Never fallen in love with him...

She'd have gone on from day to day, year to year, safe and sheltered from the wilder shores of love.

But surely, she thought, clinging to straws, surely love was never wasted? Eventually the pain must fade, and then she'd be able to live again and be glad that she'd loved him.

Still holding the flower, she went inside and put it into a tumbler of water. Cleaning up the vegetable garden had covered her in grime; sweat ran in rivulets down the back of her neck and between her breasts, and a sharp stabbing at her temple threatened her with a headache. And she still had work to do—the last of the packing, clothes to fling into a suitcase.

But first she'd shower. When she'd left Auckland the clothes Curt had bought for her remained behind; the day after they'd arrived on her doorstep courtesy of a courier van. Determined to own nothing that reminded her of him, nothing to pin hopes to, she'd refused to accept them.

Dry-eyed, she scrubbed the sweat and dirt from her body and washed her hair. She'd just rinsed the shampoo away when she heard Laddie barking again.

Now who? she thought wearily, and scrambled out of the shower, wet hair streaming down her back.

The barks tapered off as she briskly dried herself off. So it was someone she knew; a neighbour, probably. Although she hadn't announced that she was leaving the news had got around, and she'd been moved by the friendly good wishes and injunctions to 'stay in touch' she'd received.

After rubbing the towel over her head she pulled on a

cotton shirt and a pair of elderly shorts and opened the front door, pushing the wet mass of hair back from her face.

'Hello,' she said to the figure silhouetted by the brilliant glare of sunlight.

And then her eyes adjusted and she saw who it was. Her mouth dropped open and the world tilted so hideously she had to grab the doorhandle to stop herself from sliding onto the floor.

Curt said something explosive and caught her, his grip calculated to support, not hurt. 'You *are* pregnant!' he accused harshly, carrying her into the sitting room. 'And you're sick with it—you've lost far too much weight!'

'I am not!' Her heart was beating like a snare drum underneath the thin cotton shirt. 'Not pregnant and not sick. I've been busy. Put me down! I'm all right, and I'm dripping all over you.'

He set her on her feet, but retained a firm hold on her shoulders, his expression unguarded and fierce. 'You fainted.'

'No, I just got a shock—I didn't expect to s-see you.' Her tongue fumbled over the words, so she dragged in a deep breath and started again. 'What do you want?'

A perfectly reasonable question, surely, but it seemed to anger him even further. He gave her a small shake before his hands dropped to his sides. With an intensity that scared her, he said between his teeth, 'Don't lie to me, Peta. If you're carrying my child you might as well tell me here and now, because I'll find out—I'm not letting you out of my sight—'

'I told you—I'm *not*.' But oh, how she wished she were...

'I don't trust you,' he said flatly, not giving an inch.

'You're saying that because you know I'd insist on marriage.'

'I wouldn't marry you if you were the last man in the universe,' she snapped, sensation surging through a body that had miraculously, rapturously, sprung to life again. 'Will it convince you if I take a pregnancy test and *prove* there's no baby?'

Hot anger narrowed his eyes in a hooded, dangerous glare. Tension sizzled between them, naked and challenging. Several charged moments later he said more moderately, 'No, you don't have to do that. I believe you. But why have you lost weight? And you did almost faint just then.'

His concern weakened her resolution. Ignoring the first question, she said stonily, 'I've been working in the garden and I—well, I think I must be a bit dehydrated. Also I didn't expect to see you. What do you want?'

'I'll get you something to drink,' he said with another frown.

'I can get it myself—'

He started towards her. 'Peta, just shut up and let me look after you, all right?'

She retreated ahead of him; if he touched her again she'd break into several million fragments. Panicked by his inexorable progress, she finished in a voice she couldn't keep steady, 'Curt, I don't want you here. I don't need you to look after me!'

'Tough,' he said relentlessly, showing his teeth in a smile that sent ice scudding the length of her spine.

By then they'd reached the kitchen. Curt picked up the glass with the gardenia flower in it, tossed the bloom onto the counter and washed the glass out before filling it from the tap. Holding it out to her, he commanded in a tone that brooked no refusal, 'Drink.'

Peta gulped it, mind racing as she tried to work out what was going on. And behind the shock and the turmoil, her heart sang.

Curt said, 'And when you've finished drinking, you can tell me why you're not wearing a bra.'

One hand bunched the material of her shirt over her breasts, hiding them. Her pulse began to pound. 'I've just got out of a shower. I thought you were a neighbour who'd come to say goodbye.'

He came towards her with the lithe, dangerous intensity of a stalking panther. 'I see your furniture's still here.'

'The truck's picking it up tomorrow.' She swallowed and backed up a couple of steps. 'H-how did you know I'd sold?'

'Because I bought the place, of course,' he said indifferently.

'I see.' White-lipped, she stared at him. Idiot! She should have known—that explained the prompt sale, the easy agreement to anything she'd wanted, the whole smooth efficiency of the sale.

He couldn't wait to get rid of her. At that moment she hated him.

'The truck's not coming for your furniture until tomorrow?' He began to undo the buttons of his shirt, long, tanned fingers flicking them open—one, two, three...

Mesmerised, Peta fixed her eyes on the fascinating pattern of dark hair that provided such a subtle tactile contrast to his bronze skin. She licked her lips. 'What—what are you doing?'

His smile was a lazy threat. 'I'm getting ready to make love to you,' he said, and shrugged out of the shirt, letting it drop to the ground.

'No,' she croaked, but her body shouted, Yes!

And he heard it. Triumph lit his face.

Shaking her head doggedly, Peta said, 'You can persuade me, but I don't want it.'

She didn't expect to deter him, but something in her desperate tone must have rung true, because he stopped a pace away from her and examined her in dark, angry frustration.

Finally he swore in a low, self-derisive voice that made her blink, and turned away.

Scanning the powerful male wedge of his shoulders, wondering what was going on behind the hard face, Peta could only think that she had thrown away her last chance to make love with him. And although her body rebelled, she knew she couldn't make any other decision. She wanted much more from him than the quick slaking of an appetite.

She said, 'What about your lover?' The words emerged without conscious thought.

He swung back and stared at her as though she was mad. 'Lover?'

'Anna Lee,' she told him thinly, each word a stab in the heart. 'I saw the photo of you with her at polo. Does she know you're here?'

Coldly precise, he told her, 'That photograph was taken in the five minutes we spent together. Trust doesn't come easily to you, does it? I told you the relationship was off.'

'I learned not to trust from you,' she said sharply, trying to tamp down the relief that warmed her. 'It looked very much *on* in the photograph.'

He strode across to the window as though he couldn't bear to be close to her any more. 'Which just shows,' he said sardonically, 'that you should never trust a photograph.'

'You did.'

'Yes.' Still staring out of the window he said, 'I was wrong.'

Peta swallowed, but when he didn't say anything more she knew she couldn't leave it at that. Her mouth dry, she asked hoarsely, 'Curt, why are you here?'

'I came because I couldn't stay away.' Although he stood with his back to her she could hear every stony word. 'I don't know what the hell you do to me, but it reduces me to an idiot. I came here determined to court you, to show you that I wasn't some blind fool who wanted nothing more from you than mind-blowing sex. And all it took was one look at you, and my control was shot and my brain sank into some Neanderthal craving that won't let me go.'

Her pulse was thudding like a festival drum, and she didn't dare believe he'd actually said those words. Surely they were some figment of a mind that had snapped? Primly, she said into a gathering silence, 'Archaeologists seem to believe that the Neanderthals were actually peaceful people.'

He gave a short, mirthless laugh and at last turned to face her. Bewildered, she saw that the olive skin was stretched over the splendid framework of his face, and his mouth was grim.

'Peta, I've done this all wrong. Can we start over?'

Her heart shuddered to a halt, then began again, banging in her breast so that she couldn't hear her own thoughts. 'Start what?' she asked, still unable to let herself hope.

Curt's smile turned savage, then vanished, leaving his face honed into a predatory alertness. 'When you look at me it's as though you're seeing someone else. Your father?'

She had to swallow before she could say, 'I suppose so. But not always.'

'Did he abuse you?'

'*No.*' She paused, then added, 'But I've told you—he was a dominant man. Like you.'

And knew with a flash of complete certainty that it no longer mattered. She loved Curt so much that she'd take whatever risk. If he only wanted her for a few months, she'd accept that. If he wanted more—and she didn't dare probe into what 'more' might mean—she was strong enough to cope with his inbuilt authority.

Little beads of moisture forming at her temples, she swallowed. Nothing venture, she thought bravely, nothing win, but it took every ounce of courage she possessed to say, 'It's not important any more.'

'I think it is.' Brows drawing together, he looked around. 'Sit down and I'll make you some tea.'

Automatically she said, 'I'll do it.'

But while she filled the kettle and plugged it into the socket he opened the fridge door and took out milk. She got the tea caddy and teapot from the cupboard and he found the mugs; each of them, she noted as her brain buzzed in useless tumult, being exceedingly careful not to even brush up against each other.

Once seated at the dining table, mugs in front of them, he returned to the attack. 'Tell me about your father. It sounds to me as though he was a man in the grip of an obsession, prepared to sacrifice everything—even those he loved—to it.'

'That describes him fairly accurately,' she agreed, looking down into her teacup. 'The terrible thing is that I think he really did love my mother, yet he didn't seem to realise that his actions doomed her to a kind of half-life. She was a good musician—a violinist until working so hard ruined her hands. He considered it to be just a hobby, and a useless one. She loved art, but he always said that a well-grown vegetable was work of art enough for him. She loved flowers, but he said they took up time that was needed for other things. In a way he starved her of almost everything she loved, yet he couldn't see what he was doing.'

Silence stretched between them, filled with tension and unspoken thoughts. Peta almost jumped when Curt said in a voice so neutral it sounded alien, 'Is that how I seem to you? Totally self-absorbed, so lost in my own private ambitions that I have no interest in anyone else's?'

Thoughts jostled in her mind like chips of ice in a blender. 'I—no,' Peta answered, because every overbearing action of Curt's had been for his sister. Even though he didn't like Ian much, he allowed Gillian her own preferences.

'Surely your mother could have fought for her own interests?'

'She loved him and she wanted him to be happy,' she protested, yearning passionately for the sweet recklessness of desire to swamp her fears. If only he'd sweep her into his arms she'd forget everything but her own rapture.

For a while. She bit her lip. She had to think, and for once, she had to think without the hangovers from her childhood clouding her logic.

She said, 'I'm not like her, but I think I understand how she felt.'

He said keenly, 'You're afraid, Peta, of something— that's been obvious right from the start. You've called me a dominant man several times, as though that's the worst insult you can hurl at me. But you're certainly not afraid of me; you've stood up against me without quailing.'

'Of course I'm not scared of you,' she retorted. 'It's myself—' She stopped, suddenly wary, unsure of what she'd intended to say. How could she be afraid of herself? Ridiculous!

Determination hardened his face; he wasn't going to let her off easily. 'Is that what scares you? Not fear of being dominated, but fear of falling in love? Because your mother didn't have the strength to stand up for herself—and you—you don't dare let yourself fall in love in case it turns you into a weakling?'

When she didn't answer he smiled with hard irony. 'Look at yourself, my darling! Nobody could ride roughshod over you because you wouldn't let them. I tried, and failed lamentably. You're strong.'

'I don't know what you're talking about,' she muttered.

But a shadow she'd lived under all her life lifted from her. Picking her way through her thoughts, she went on, 'The police said there was no reason for the accident that killed my parents; an onlooker said the car suddenly sped up, then swerved and smashed straight into the concrete power pole.'

He covered her hand with his big one, warming her from the inside. She took in a deep, shuddering breath and went on, 'I think he realised that Mum hadn't mentioned the symptoms of her illness because she was afraid of—oh, of not living up to his standards. And he couldn't bear it. The police said he might have gone to sleep at the wheel, but he never slept in the daytime. I think he drove into that pole deliberately and killed them both so that he didn't have to live with himself.'

Curt swore quietly, but he didn't touch her. 'No wonder you were so damned cautious.' He paused before adding deliberately, 'Do you really believe that love entails surrender and endless sacrifice, the complete subjugation of one person's will to another's?'

'Love?' she whispered, unable to believe that he'd used the word.

He didn't move. 'If what I feel isn't love,' he said in a flat, toneless voice, 'I don't ever want to feel the real thing. Of course I love you! You smashed through my control, turned my life upside down, scrambled my brains so that I made love to you when I knew it was more dangerous than anything I'd ever done. And when you left it ripped my heart from my body and all light from life. My executives think I'm losing it and my poor PA is at her wits' end because she has to remind me about every meeting. My house is haunted by your lovely, challenging ghost. When I smell the gardenias outside you come to me, and I want you so much I can't breathe.'

Peta's eyes burned with unshed tears. 'I know,' she confessed. 'It's like living in a grey limbo.'

More than anything she wanted the inestimable comfort of his arms, the magical euphoria of being held close to him, but he stayed on the other side of the table, linked to her only by his hand tightening around hers.

'So how do you feel about me?' he asked, his voice unnaturally level.

She looked up sharply, and read naked hope in his eyes; incredulously she realised he needed the words too. 'You must know I love you,' she said simply. 'With everything I am, all that I can be.'

And at last he got to his feet and she rose with him and went to him.

'How could you not know?' she asked, trembling as his arms closed around her.

'How could you not?' Tantalising, confident, his mouth touched the corner of hers in a butterfly kiss that sank into the depths of her soul like rain after a long, dry summer.

The soft, purring noise in the back of her throat surprised her; smiling, she lifted her hands and lovingly shaped his face, holding his head still as she looked into burning eyes that promised her everything.

This time his kiss won a passionate response, her mouth parting beneath the hard demand of his, her body exulting in the evidence of his fierce arousal and the wonder of being close to him again, of loving him.

Tremors raked her body when he lifted his head.

'God,' he muttered against her lips. 'I love you so much I'd kill for you. I've spent the last month eating my heart out, lying in bed at night and aching for you, obsessing over the way you look when you smile, when you laugh, when you frown, remembering how sweet and fiery and passionate you were, and how much I enjoy crossing swords with you...'

She closed his mouth with hers, and he lifted her up and swung her into his arms and carried her into the bedroom. As he lowered her to the bed he said, 'I need you so much, my darling heart. So much.'

It was like a vow. She drew his head down to her, and with a smile trembling on her lips said, 'We could probably spend hours discussing who needs who most, but— not now?'

Curt laughed deep in his throat. 'Not now,' he agreed, and came down beside her and slowly, with love and passion and tenderness, they came together.

Much later, when she was lying naked in his arms and he was exploring her body with his fingertips, producing a shivering delight with the lightest touch, he said, 'What's wrong?'

Peta didn't try to gloss it over. 'I can't help wondering what Gillian is going to think of—of us.'

'She'll be too busy patching up her marriage and organising an adoption to worry too much.' When she frowned he said, 'We had a long talk after my father's funeral. I hope I managed to convince her that she owes it to herself to do something with her art. After they got home she had another long discussion with Ian; she thinks everything is going to be all right now. She's decided to stop aiming for the sun and take what she can.'

'That's so sad!' she burst out, because she had aimed for her sun and struck home, and she wanted everyone to be as happy as she was. After all, if it hadn't been for Ian and Gillian, she might never have met Curt...

Curt kissed her forehead. She shivered deliciously at the heated slide of his skin over hers, the sensuous friction rekindling the fires she'd thought sated.

'I may not agree with the way she chooses to live, but it's her decision to make,' he said quietly. 'Besides, my marriage is my own affair. My mother is waiting for us to set a date—what have I said?'

Peta stared into his face, saw a blazing purpose that thrilled her even as it scared her.

He said quietly, 'You are going to marry me, aren't you, Peta?'

Happiness collided with astonishment. 'I didn't think... marriage? Curt, are you sure?'

He bent his head and kissed the pleading tip of one breast. 'I'm not going to settle for anything else, so I'll just have to dazzle you with sex until you finally give in,' he said, his breath playing across the moist skin with unnerving eroticism. 'You're not thinking of my father's unsubtle attempt to manipulate things, are you? It was so bloody typical of him—he had no idea how to deal with people! He guessed, of course, that I was in love with you, and he wanted to make things easier.' He gave an exasperated laugh. 'Or something.'

'No, your father's got nothing to do with it,' she murmured, inwardly shuddering with anticipation so keen it held her on a knife-edge of pleasure. 'I'm not taking the money, anyway.'

His head came up, eyes narrowed to slivers of electric blue. With lips that barely moved, he exclaimed, 'What?'

'Didn't you know?' Astonishment blossomed into joy. 'I sent a letter off as soon as I got back from Auckland, refusing the legacy.'

'No, I didn't know—I've got nothing to do with his estate.'

And then she knew what real happiness was, because he had come for her even though he'd thought she'd taken the money.

Curt said, 'Peta, why? Did you think—?'

Lips trembling, she whispered, 'I'm not capable of thinking anything right now, if you really want to know.'

'Good.' But before he took her back to the enchanted realm of his love, he looked at her with a dangerous smile. 'If you don't want the money we'll form a trust in your name and use it to help people onto their own farms or something. But whatever you decide, I plan to settle more than that on you so that you have the independence you need.'

'No!' she protested, trying to pull away. Eyes enormous and troubled, she stared at his beloved face. 'I don't want it. All I'll ever want, all I'll ever need, is for you to love me.'

'That's a given. Always. But you need freedom,' he said implacably, adding with a laugh deep in his throat, 'I'll tie you to me every way I can, but money of your own will give you options and choices. You can do anything, be anything you want; all *I* want is for you to be happy.'

'I don't know how to live in your world.'

'You'll cope,' he said confidently. 'And you'll have my mother and me to help you, as well as Lucia Radcliffe.'

Peta surrendered, happiness gilding her eyes, glowing from her skin, curving her lips into a smile that shook him to the core. 'I'll be happy if I have you,' she vowed, and linked her arms around his neck and kissed him with the pent-up ardour of a lifetime.

'Perhaps after fifty years I'll be able to manage to make love to you with some finesse,' he said thickly.

'I don't care,' she said languorously, her eyes sultry and provocative. 'You may have noticed that I'm not much into finesse myself.'

Before the honeyed tide of passion overcame them, she thought that although Curt would always be dominant, he balanced it with compassion and integrity. With him she'd be safe.

And he would be safe with her...

Get *Sweet Revenge* from

PENNY JORDAN

this month and save money!

SAVE 50p

on *Sweet Revenge*
by Penny Jordan

Valid only until 31st June 2005

9 904170 570503

To the consumer: This coupon can be redeemed for £0.50 off *Sweet Revenge* by Penny Jordan at any retail store in the UK. Only one coupon can be used per purchase. Not valid for Reader Service™ books.

To the retailer: Harlequin Mills & Boon will redeem this coupon for £0.50 provided only that it has been used against the purchase of *Sweet Revenge* by Penny Jordan. Harlequin Mills & Boon reserve the right to refuse payment against misused coupons. Please submit coupons to NCH, Corby, Northants NN17 1NN.

SAVE 75c

on *Sweet Revenge*
by Penny Jordan

Valid only until 31st June 2005

9 823346 050758

To the consumer: This coupon can be redeemed for €0.75 off *Sweet Revenge* by Penny Jordan at any retail store in Eire. Only one coupon can be used per purchase. Not valid for Reader Service™ books.

To the retailer: Harlequin Mills & Boon will redeem this coupon for €0.75 provided only that it has been used against the purchase of *Sweet Revenge* by Penny Jordan. Harlequin Mills & Boon reserve the right to refuse payment against misused coupons. Please submit coupons to NCH, Corby, Northants NN17 1NN.

A very special

Mother's Day

Margaret Way
Anne Herries

*Indulge all of your romantic
senses with these two
brand-new stories...*

On sale 18th February 2005

*Available at most branches of WHSmith, Tesco, ASDA, Martins, Borders,
Eason, Sainsbury's and all good paperback bookshops.*

FREE!

4 Books
and a surprise gift!

We would like to take this opportunity to thank you for reading this Mills & Boon® book by offering you the chance to take FOUR more specially selected titles from the Modern Romance™ series absolutely FREE! We're also making this offer to introduce you to the benefits of the Reader Service™—

- ★ **FREE home delivery**
- ★ **FREE gifts and competitions**
- ★ **FREE monthly Newsletter**
- ★ **Exclusive Reader Service offers**
- ★ **Books available before they're in the shops**

Accepting these FREE books and gift places you under no obligation to buy, you may cancel at any time, even after receiving your free shipment. Simply complete your details below and return the entire page to the address below. You don't even need a stamp!

YES! Please send me 4 free Modern Romance books and a surprise gift. I understand that unless you hear from me, I will receive 6 superb new titles every month for just £2.75 each, postage and packing free. I am under no obligation to purchase any books and may cancel my subscription at any time. The free books and gift will be mine to keep in any case.

P5ZEF

Ms/Mrs/Miss/Mr ....Initials ....
BLOCK CAPITALS PLEASE

Surname ....

Address ....

....

....Postcode ....

Send this whole page to:
UK: FREEPOST CN81, Croydon, CR9 3WZ